Her Viking Dragon Warrior

Viking Ancestors
Age of Embers
Book Two

Sky Purington

Story Overview

Upon arrival at her Winter Harbor Maine rental, Athena knows it holds secrets. A mystery to figure out. Something worth discovering, she is convinced will help many. Or so she thinks until the path to a bright new future leads her straight into the arms of a ruthless warrior and a destructive past.

Viking dragon warrior Týr Sigdir has long fought to keep his people safe as unrest grows in his surrounding kingdoms. Battled until he knew little else but warfare and protecting others. That is until his most favored sword and shield find their way into the hands of a woman living a thousand years in his future. Someone who will, against all odds, challenge his need to protect anyone but her. More daunting still, an uptight yet sinfully beautiful scientist who will lead him into the dark underbelly of Scandinavia's ancient mountains.

Thrust together on a treacherous yet passionate adventure, Athena's curiosity soon puts them in the line of fire from an enemy with no face. A nemesis determined to stop them from discovering something that will make all the difference for dragonkind's fate. Will they succeed on their quest despite their foe's growing power over Athena? Or will Týr end their journey and steal her away first, risking the future of their kind to keep her safe?

Pronunciations

Åse (or-sah)
Athena (ah-thene-ah)
Helheim (hel-himm)
Jørn (yorn)
Mea (me-ah)
Mektig kriger (mek-tay krye-ger)
Midgard (mid-gard)
Múspellsheimr (moo-spell-shay-mm)
Níðhöggr (neathe-högr or neathe-herd)
Rune (roon)
Týr (tee-er)
Yggdrasil (ig-dris-ul)

Introduction

A generation after the Great War was won, the Age of Embers has begun, and unrest once again grows between the dragon kingdoms of tenth-century Norway. Some kingdoms recognize Viking Dragon King Ulrik Sigdir as their one true liege, whereas others rally against him. To make matters worse, a plague has befallen female dragons, threatening the future of dragonkind.

Or so it seemed until twenty-first-century Keira traveled back in time and mated with Ulrik, bringing hope not just via her pregnancy but a secret alliance with one of the enemies, King Knud. Since then, Ulrik's faithful subject and ruler in his own right, Týr Sigdir, has been losing his weapons across time to a woman named Athena, implying another dragonly connection is forming that could aid in the cause. And so the story goes...

Prologue

"DUCK!" A DEEP masculine voice roared, and she did, only for a chunk of molten rock to soar over her head and crash down in front of her.

She dodged left and right, but they were slamming down everywhere, crashing into the ground in an array of fiery terror and cloying smoke. Booming down in a sea of flames and explosions that grew closer and closer to the vulnerable village below.

This was *not* supposed to be happening yet.

It had come too soon.

"I should have known," she gasped. "I thought I did."

Why, though? How could she have known? Nobody could know. Yet she should have. She was convinced of it. Certain yet clearly not certain at all.

Rather, she had been fatally wrong.

"No," she roared. "I can't be wrong!"

She had been, though, because the mountain's summit exploded with fire. Glorious, wonderful, lethal fire. Stunning flames of such sheer beauty, she nearly smiled until she remembered how many would die at its hands.

How it had been her duty to keep them safe.

Him safe.

And she still could. Would. *Had* to.

"Stop," he roared from somewhere behind her. "You cannot stop it now. You cannot—"

He said more, but she couldn't hear it as she raced toward the summit of the towering, angry mountain. Dodged around smoking, dangerous projectiles. Flew upward, determined to stop something that was unstoppable, but she had to try. Had to do something because she had failed them, *him*, so miserably.

How to fight it, though?

How to extinguish the mightiest of fires when, deep down, she was infatuated with it? Had, perhaps, somehow willed it to her even as she tried to keep it away?

"Yet I can hold it back," she swore, racing uphill through thick, black smoke and flaming trees. "I can…have to…"

Could she, though?

Did she have that kind of strength?

Would she survive it?

"Stop!" the same masculine voice from behind roared again, calling to her in a heartbreaking way she couldn't quite understand. "Don't go!"

Almost as if his anguished plea invoked it, a fiery circle arose toward the summit. Within the circle, an orange and red shield with back-to-back dragons.

Back-to-back warriors.

That was it. The shield that would protect all.

Her only hope at redemption.

At saving everything that mattered most.

2

So she raced toward it, determined to grab it. Use it. Instead, when she reached out, she clasped the hilt of a sword. A blade, as it happened, that she thrust into the last place she expected.

A place that made no sense at all.

-Her Viking Dragon Warrior-

Chapter One

Winter Harbor, Maine
Present Day

"STOP," ATHENA CRIED and thrust her sword into the chest of the hazy, not-quite-there Viking who haunted her before he gripped her shoulders and shook her so hard, she jolted awake only to find someone else entirely staring back at her.

Quinn frowned down with a furrowed brow. "Are you *really* awake this time, Athena?"

"What?" she croaked around a bone-dry throat and struggled to sit up.

Where was he?

Where was *she?*

What happened?

She blinked at her blurry friend until Quinn put Athena's glasses on, and she snapped into focus. "Where am I?"

"Where you've been for a few days now," Quinn said, gently urging her to lie back down. She had her blond bob clipped back and looked more than a little strained around her thickly lashed, deep green eyes. "Caught between nearly killing a perfect stranger and...this..."

"This being what?" she asked weakly, taking in a bedroom that became more familiar by the moment. "I'm still here," she whispered, half caught in her fading nightmare and the room she'd claimed at the chalet she and her friends had rented for the winter. "Even though I was just somewhere else..."

"Ya think?" Quinn worked at a teasing smile before her finely arched brows bunched. "So, are you back for sure this time? Because I could really use you around...all of us could."

The tentative way Quinn said that last part made her tense. "All of who? Are Zoey and Savannah here already?"

"Zoey, yes." Quinn shook her head. "But not Savannah." Her eye color flickered from the dark green she was born with to a lighter shade of green to match the plant on the table behind her, signifying her dragon magic hovered right beneath the surface. "And of course, Rune's still here and, well..."

"Well, what?" she prompted, frowning. A chill raced up her spine. "Who else is here?"

"Him." Quinn flinched. "The one you nearly ran through with a sword when you were—"

"*No*," she gasped, mortified. Athena batted Quinn away when she urged her to lie down again. "Impossible." She shook her head and prayed she was still dreaming. "You can't mean—" she swallowed hard when his scarred face flashed in her mind again— "he isn't *real*."

He couldn't be. Better not be.

Yet, based on the scattered dreams she'd been having, somehow she feared he was.

"Oh, trust me, Týr's real." Quinn seemed to weigh her words carefully. "And eager to meet you again."

"Real like...how real?" She eyed her friend warily. "I've been having strange dreams, and then there's Rune's tea." She narrowed her eyes. "What's with our landlord, anyway? She's a different sort, isn't she?"

Every time Rune handed Athena a cup of tea since arriving at the chalet, she meant to turn it away because it tended to make her black out, yet unable to help herself, she took a sip of the delicious brew anyway. Not good, considering she'd given up alcohol years ago because a little bit tended to go a long way with her.

"Wow, how much have you forgotten?" Quinn narrowed her eyes and tilted her head. "You recall Rune's a demi-god seer from tenth-century Norway, right? She's super powerful and likely spiked your tea with magic?"

"Um, I sort of remember." Honestly, it all seemed pretty hazy. Most definitely dreamlike. She pinched the bridge of her nose and tried to focus on the foggy dreams that had come and gone, yet his, *Týr's*, face kept rising to the top.

A terrifying Viking with vicious eyes.

A demon's face surrounded by endless lethal weapons.

"*Sort* of remember?" Quinn echoed, growing more worried. She handed Athena a glass of water that had been sitting on the bedside table and urged her to drink to ease her dry throat. "What about Keira? You recall everything she's been through since traveling back in time, right?"

"Keira?" she said softly, sipping the water.

Something about Quinn mentioning her best friend brought back bits and pieces. How Keira traveled back in time and hooked up with a Viking dragon king named Ulrik on a mission to save dragonkind, then ended up with his enemy. She also recalled King Ulrik showing up to grill Rune about what she knew about Keira because he was determined to save her.

"Oh, no," she whispered, widening her eyes at Quinn when she recalled spinning in merriment borne of Rune's tea only to nearly drive a towering Viking through the chest with a sword.

Týr's sword she found in the living room surrounded by *his* weapons.

It seemed Rune had cast some kind of spell that made Keira and Athena see different things on the walls downstairs. Fortunately for Keira, Athena seeing Týr's weapons meant Keira's fate with the enemy wasn't cut in stone. Unfortunately, it also likely meant Athena was supposed to help Týr in some unknown way.

Big, bad biker-looking Týr.

She had been convinced when she first pulled up to this house that she would discover something remarkable. Something to help mankind. Now this. *Him.* And undoubtedly, plenty of terrifying medieval violence to go along with it.

"I remember enough," Athena managed, finally responding to Quinn. Vaguely recalling King Ulrik's concern for Keira when he and his friends had shown up in their living room, she cocked her head at Quinn. "Has Keira returned? Did Ulrik save her?"

"He *did*," Quinn said carefully, clearly trying to go about this just the right way. "And she's okay. In fact, they got married and are, no doubt, waiting for you in the distant past."

"Married?" she mouthed, not as surprised as she might have been, given she'd felt how strong Ulrik and Keira's connection was. Still.

Married to a Viking dragon over a thousand years in the past? That was huge, but by no means what alarmed her most. "What do you mean they're waiting for me in the distant past?"

"She means Queen Keira is waiting for you to travel back in time so you can show me where you hid my damn shield, woman," came an all-too-familiar telepathic voice. *"So make haste because I want it back."*

She both cringed and shivered with a strange sort of awareness at the deep rumble in her mind. One she had heard before in her dreams. A voice she was fairly certain she had communicated with across time while in one of her Rune-induced tea states.

"Oh, no, no, no," she said under her breath. Sensing Týr on the other side of her bedroom door, she scrambled that way and rested her back against it to keep him from entering.

"Go away," she called out loud enough for him to hear. "I'm not going anywhere with you."

"Ja, you are," he growled from the hallway outside, speaking good enough English. *"Now."*

"This is crazy," she seethed softly at Quinn. She eyed the windows, wondering if she could escape that way, but they were too high up. Especially for a dragon that had never embraced her inner beast. "What am I supposed to do?"

"I would begin by trying to reason with him." Quinn gave her a sympathetic smile that didn't ease her fear any. "Because he's not budging." She shook her head. "He hasn't once in nearly two days that I know of, although he must've overnight for obvious reasons."

"You let him stand outside my door all that time?" she exclaimed. "Seriously?"

"Have you seen the size of him?" Quinn raised her hand in the air to signify his substantial height, then spanned her hands in

9

front of her, indicating the width of his shoulders. "He might look a little less fierce now, thanks to Rune, but that doesn't make him any less a solid wall of...well, *man*."

Was her friend blushing? She couldn't be. Athena had seen Týr, and he was terrifying. Not attractive in the least. A feral beast who might be half man but seemed all dragon.

On top of that, Quinn tended to have exemplary taste when it came to men. Her boyfriends were always ridiculously attractive, but Quinn, with her auburn-streaked blond bob-cut shorter in the back than the front and her tall, willowy frame and stunning features, looked like a supermodel herself, so not surprising. Men considered Quinn a solid ten out of ten, and while she wasn't superficial by any means, she tended to be attracted to men equally gorgeous.

Therefore, her thinking Týr was attractive made no sense.

"Ah, there you are," Zoey exclaimed with a warm smile, taking matters out of Athena's hands when she chanted the door away and embraced her. "I was getting worried you were going to sleep right through winter."

"*Sorry, but chances were slim to none that you were ever coming out of your room,*" Zoey said telepathically. "*And only a matter of time before Týr's patience snapped, so best to face all this directly.*"

Directly? Was she insane?

Typically, Zoey, diplomat that she was, would have talked Athena out of her room, but it seemed everything was out of whack because she'd just used dragon magic despite swearing it off years ago. They had all sworn it off when they'd joined an online support group called Fire Anonymous for dragons. Basically, it was for dragon misfits who struggled with their inner beast's natural element. Either they loved or hated it too much to be considered a proper dragon.

As it happened, Athena liked it too much, hence becoming a volcanologist.

She realized why Zoey had used magic so readily when she locked eyes on the giant standing nonchalantly against the balcony railing opposite Athena's bedroom door. Týr might not be dressed like a Viking anymore, but he was still ridiculously imposing and a threat to anyone with two eyes. Moreover, he could easily kick down a door with his pinky finger if he wanted to.

Simmering potential for violence aside, he cleaned up surprisingly well in black jeans, boots, and an equally dark sweater that did nothing to hide his muscular build and impossibly broad shoulders.

The first time she'd seen him, his hair was shaved closer to the scalp on either side of his head, and his weaved braids were pulled together from his forehead down past his shoulder blades. Now, his style was loose and less primal looking. His beard was as black as his attire, but his ebony hair was highlighted with dark brown and blond highlights. Where she'd only seen the scar that cut from his forehead and inner right brow, down his cheek to his bearded jawline before, now she noticed the deep-set, mysterious cobalt blue of his thickly lashed eyes.

More so, the intense way those eyes took her in.

She felt the anger churning in his steady gaze but also felt something else.

Something odd and unusual.

"That's called attraction, love," Rune purred, clearly catching Athena's thoughts as she sauntered down the hallway overlooking the massive living room. The seer stopped beside Týr—who had his arms crossed over his chest— and smiled demurely at him. "Which is good considering he will have no other but you despite his inner Helheim attracting all in his presence."

Inner Helheim? As in one of the nine worlds in Norse mythology?

And what was that about him only having Athena?

Even if she was a teensy tiny bit attracted to him now, despite him being nowhere near her type, she couldn't hold a candle to Quinn and Zoey in the looks department. Quinn was just Quinn, and Zoey wasn't too far off with her silky straight blue-black hair, petite, delicate frame, exotic oriental features, and mesmerizing turquoise eyes. If the two of them didn't make a man drool, there was always Rune with her long, luxurious ebony hair and exquisite looks, who only seemed to grow more beautiful the longer one knew her.

Then there was Athena.

She had long gotten over thinking she would never be as pretty as other women with her too-curvy body, rather plain features, and terrible eyesight that needed special glasses. So, instead of worrying about her appearance, she'd focused on her love of science. Men in her field tended to care less about a woman's looks and more about her mind, so it worked. *She* worked. And tirelessly at that. Most would probably call her a workaholic.

Not to say she didn't like to date when she came across her type. For that matter, she'd done just that and finally asked her neighbor out. Better still, he had accepted and was supposed to meet her here in Winter Harbor in a few days.

Oh. Dear. God.

"What day is it?" she whispered in Zoey's ear in case Týr could catch her inner dialogue with her friends. "Tell me it's not Friday."

"Why?" Zoey pulled back and frowned, getting that look she always got when she sensed her peacekeeping skills might be put to the test more than they already were. "What's going on?"

"Nothing." She shook her head, pushed her glasses up her nose, and tried not to wring her hands. "I need my phone so I can call—"

"Here you go, darling." Rune handed it to her as if she knew this moment was coming. One black brow swept up. "Although I suspect it is too late."

"Too late for what?" Zoey asked as the doorbell rang.

"That I would say." Rune eyed Týr with a small, knowing smile. "See, I told you it was best you dress for this century." She clasped her hands together in delight. "Just imagine how awkward having company would have been otherwise?"

"What company?" Zoey and Quinn said simultaneously, their inner dragons in sync.

"John," Athena groaned, mortified when she realized she wore nothing but baggy sweats and, her cheeks flamed, no *bra*. She wouldn't have dressed like this in front of her friends, never mind a Viking dragon from the past.

"Who?" Zoey asked.

"John, my neighbor turned friend turned potential...oh, never mind." She shook her head and shoved Zoey along. "Please tell him I'll meet him outside in a few minutes."

Meanwhile, rather than glance Týr's way and suffer more embarrassment, she yanked Quinn back into her bedroom and chanted the door back in place, surprised by how strange using her magic felt after all this time.

"How did I get into these clothes!" She flew to the closet and tore through her tidily hung conservative clothing, frowning all the while. "And who took off my *bra?*" She stopped and rounded her eyes at Quinn when a horrifying thought occurred to her. "Did Týr...tell me he didn't...*see* anything..."

13

"He didn't see anything," Quinn assured. "According to Rune, he left soon after you thrust his sword at his chest, and you passed out...then I passed out because of Rune's magic. When you didn't rouse along with me shortly after, Rune realized you were reacting to Týr being here, so she dressed you in what she felt would be most comfortable and got you into bed."

"What kind of reaction to Týr?" Curious when she should be angry for being duped with magic, she pushed her glasses up her nose again and thought like a scientist. "Hives? An allergic reaction of some sort?"

That would make sense, considering she *did* have occasional allergies, and he came from not only a place she'd never been but another whole era, so who knows what was growing back then.

"Um, not quite hives." Quinn again trod carefully with well-selected words. "More like...a chemical reaction brought on by your dragon, as Rune put it. A feverish response having to do with heightened awareness rather than an allergic reaction."

When Athena frowned at her because she wasn't following, Quinn shrugged and finally spoke bluntly. "Evidently, you were aroused, sweetie. Or, better put, your inner dragon was."

She went to deny that possibility when Zoey cut into their conversation telepathically with damning words. *You might want to hurry up, Athena. I'm not sure how he managed it, but Týr got to the door before me.*

Chapter Two

TÝR HAD WANTED to shake Athena awake for the better part of two days, but whenever he managed to get past her friends when they finally slept, he just couldn't do it. Instead, he mostly stared down at her and clenched his fists in frustration because she affected him so strangely. For the first time in his life, he felt helpless when it came to doing what he must.

In this case, retrieve his most favored weapons.

Weapons his parents had given him when he was very young. He'd since learned they had been given to them by the god Loki, with a message that if they ever found their way into the hands of another against Týr's will, then there was more to King Ulrik's story than they anticipated. More alarmingly, Týr might very well be tied to a woman from the future, just like his father before him.

Now, he was chasing his weapons around in time, and while he had retrieved his sword from Athena, she had hidden his shield somewhere in a volcanic Norwegian mountain. Or so she claimed in one of her Rune-tea drunken declarations. Either way, there was little he could do until she woke outside of scooping her up, bringing her back to his lair, and forcing her awake.

Yet he could not seem to do it.

Not when she looked so peaceful. So mesmerizingly beautiful and untouchable resting. Her hair wasn't pulled back into a tight bun with a stubborn flyaway or two like it had been before but fanned around her face on the pillow in a thick, luxurious cascade of mahogany-tinted ebony locks.

And what a face.

Upon first meeting Athena when she thrust his sword at his chest, her lovely features had been swallowed up by unfortunate, thick, black-rimmed glasses that made her blue eyes appear blurry and unnaturally large.

Not anymore, though.

He had wondered what she'd looked like without glasses and was by no means disappointed. Her skin was olive-toned and flawless, and her features captivating and lovely. Her lips were fuller than he was used to on a woman, and they kept drawing his eye. Tempted him in ways that made him want to taste them when, typically, outside of his partner, Åse, he didn't bother with kissing. It served no purpose when it came to the needs of his cock, which generally, if well cared for, kept his personality level.

Or at least that's how things were until Athena started summoning his weapons to her across time. Ulrik had retrieved Týr's prized blade when he traveled here, but yet again, it returned to Athena along with many other blades. They made their way back to a woman who somehow seduced him even as she slept.

Not just with the beauty of her face, either, but with the ample curves of a body he hadn't been able to see when she was covered with a down comforter but saw clearly enough when she pulled away from Zoey's embrace the next day. Rune might have put

Athena into overly large clothes, but they did little to disguise her lush curves.

Her full, well-rounded breasts.

Considering his cock hadn't worked properly since he heard Athena's voice in his mind, it was a wonder he didn't take her right then and there. A miracle when it swelled with approval, more than willing to sink inside her. Fortunately, his mood wasn't quite as foul as it could be at the moment, so he didn't need her out of necessity. Rather, he felt somewhat at ease for the first time in his life and could take his time because he *would* eventually have her.

Or so he thought until the doorbell rang, and his inner beast came to attention. With good reason, too, given Athena's reaction and what he sensed flitting through her mind.

A man she wanted was at the door.

Not a dragon but a flesh and blood mortal man.

Zoey didn't stand a chance of getting to the door first when Týr chanted himself there in a split second. In no mood to let anyone near Athena, let alone someone who thought to take his place between her thighs, he went to open the door only to find himself sitting on the couch with a chilled bottle of ale in hand as Rune opened the door and greeted the newcomer.

"Damn seer," he cursed, only for Rune to seethe into his mind that he better be on his best behavior lest they have this century's police descend on them because he had slain Athena's man where he stood.

"*Think about it, Týr—*" Rune went on telepathically, talking to him like they were still children, and he was out of control once again— "*setting aside your lust for Athena, you want your shield back, yes? Ja? If you cut this man down, you risk not only trouble with the authorities but will inevitably lose any trust you hope to gain from Athena.*" She paused, letting that sink in. "*You adjusted your appearance as I requested, and look what a difference that made in how Athena looks at you, so I can be trusted.*"

"*Can you?*" he wondered. "*Because as far as I can tell, and as Ulrik claimed, you are a trickster. Not to be trusted entirely because he suspects you loved the enemy's son at one time. The dragon prince's brother, Jørn. King Knud's son.*"

"*An enemy no longer,*" she reminded even as her sultry voice greeted Athena's man further down the hallway. "*As it were, has King Ulrik not made a peace pact with King Knud, father to the prince and his brother?*"

"*A peace pact that has nothing to do with his sons nor your actions of the past,*" he returned, not about to let Rune free of guilt because of Ulrik's good judgment.

In truth, they remained in the dark about Rune's suspected dalliance with Jørn, only that it was over now and the seer, however obtuse and devious, was here to protect the chalet's inhabitants. Or so Ulrik was convinced. Therefore, Týr would accept it until he witnessed something that led him to believe otherwise.

"Come in and sit, John," Rune said aloud, her voice deceptively welcoming.

Zoey shot Týr a warning glance to behave, then smiled warmly from her perch in the kitchen at the slight-framed man wearing crooked eyeglasses and carrying a worn brown leather briefcase. There was little to him other than painfully over-combed dull brown hair and a bit more height than most men of this era. He certainly didn't possess the ability to fight or defend others, nor by any means could he truly appreciate a woman like Athena, which made him pointless in Týr's eyes.

"Hi." Zoey's smile grew warmer still as she introduced herself and Týr. When she claimed Týr was her friend, he corrected her and said he was here for Athena, leaving what that meant open to interpretation.

"Would you like something to drink, John?" Zoey said, clearly intent on breaking the awkward silence as John eyed Týr uneasily. "We have just about everything."

"Black coffee would be nice," John replied, his voice predictably cracking under the warning glare Týr had long perfected when facing off with too many combatants to count. A look that told his Soon To Be Slain opponents their battle was lost before it had even begun.

Setting aside Týr was by far the superior warrior, he sensed John's heart rate increasing with heightened nerves. A typical reaction when human men were around dragon males, whether they realized what they were or not. Much like prey sensing a predator, his was the same reaction a human might get if a lion stalked into the room, eyeing them with bared teeth and a low growl. Unfortunately for the other man, Týr was no mere lion, and John was a threat. Even more of one when Athena joined them, and John's pulse raced at the sight of her.

Týr nearly manifested a dagger and whipped it straight into his heart so it knew better than to beat for her but clenched his fist instead because Rune was right. If he cut John down too soon, he would lose Athena's trust, putting her and his shield out of reach.

Yet how tempted he was if for no other reason than how Athena blushed when she smiled hello at John. Her tempting breasts might be hidden under a stiff brown blazer, her hair once again in a bun, and her overall appearance transformed to promote less allure, but Týr still saw the seductress beneath.

More importantly, he saw the dragon.

One that sensed his inner beast more by the moment.

19

"Please, John." Rune gestured at the sizeable tan leather sofa across from Týr's couch. "Sit and relax. I'm sure it was a long drive in this snowy weather."

"Thank you." John smiled nervously at Athena when she sat beside him. "The roads were slick, but it was worth the commute."

Týr imagined it was. After all, he had traveled over a thousand years to get to her. Although tempted to sit between them, he downed half his ale instead and kept a close eye on John. To hell with Rune's warning. One wrong move, and it would be over for him.

"*And over for you, too,*" Quinn reminded telepathically. She sat beside Týr and smiled at John. "*Athena hates violence, so that would be it. She would never let you close again and forget about your shield.*"

He had been surprised by how comfortable Quinn and Zoey had been around him over the past few days, but then it seemed they were likely as tied in with what was happening back home as Keira and Athena. At least Quinn, who he thought would align well with his cousin, Rafe. Though her personality seemed more lighthearted than his mystic cousin, the two shared a notable affinity for nature.

Either way, both women had talked with him while he waited for Athena to wake. Quinn seemed open, kind, and optimistic, whereas Zoey was more reserved. She questioned him more than Quinn and was determined to understand as much as she could about the various kingdoms of his homeland and their longstanding blood feuds.

"As asked, I brought the results from your samples, Athena." John gestured at the briefcase he had rested by his foot. "I'll admit, they're very interesting." Clearly unsure what to say, he eyed her tentatively. "Should I assume they're some sort of joke?"

"Samples?" Athena asked blankly, having more memory issues than any of them realized. All except Rune, undoubtedly.

"Yes, samples, love." Rune gave John his coffee before Zoey had a chance to. "Before you bumped your head, you were busy taking samples of almost everything around here, Athena."

"Oh, I didn't realize…" John looked at Athena with concern. "I'm so sorry. Are you okay?"

"I am," Athena said slowly, offering a weak smile. "Just a minor bump."

"What is he talking about?" she asked everyone telepathically, or so it seemed because Týr heard her as well. And once again, her internal voice made his inner beast come to attention.

Made everything come to attention, for that matter.

Rune responded as Athena sipped from a glass of water she brought downstairs, reminding her she'd not only taken samples of just about everything on the property but had become particularly interested in the ashes on the hearth. In addition, according to Athena herself, at some point, she had hidden Týr's shield in either an active or inactive volcano somewhere in Norway.

When Athena nearly choked on her water, Zoey moved to her other side and patted her back.

"Before you fell on the ice and bumped your head, Athena—" Rune went on, saying anything that would make sense to the scrawny interloper who could barely take his eyes off Athena— "I believe you mentioned something about sending samples off to your friend, John, so he could have them tested."

"Did I then?" Athena managed, still coughing a little. Her wary yet undeniably interested gaze fell to John's briefcase. "Why didn't you just email them to me?"

"You said you didn't want them online," John reminded, nervously glancing from Týr to Athena. "You also said it would be a good opportunity to get to know one another better. That you would be interested in going out for dinner." He cleared his throat but managed to speak rather bravely, all things considered. "Should I assume that's changed?"

"Yes." In no mood for any of this, Týr downed the rest of his ale and made things clear with just enough warning in his voice. "When Athena leaves, it will be with me, not you."

"I'm so sorry, John. Please ignore him." Even though her cheeks turned rosy with either embarrassment or perhaps feisty defiance, Athena kept her gaze firmly on John. "I barely know him." Before the other man could respond, she gestured at the briefcase, eager to change the subject. "May I look at the results?"

"Of course." Without a doubt, sensing how close Týr was to coming to blows with him, John kept eyeing him nervously as he offered Athena a jerky nod and handed her a folder he pulled out of his briefcase.

"Thank you." Athena opened it and scanned sheet after sheet with growing confusion. "This can't be right." She kept reading and shook her head. "These results are impossible."

"Of course, they are because..." John began and cleared his throat. When he spoke again, his voice slurred, and his eyes glazed and began to drift. "Like you said..."

Rune swooped in and removed his coffee from his slackening grip before he slumped back against the couch and passed out.

Figuring out he'd been magically sleep-induced via his coffee, Athena's eyes rounded from John to Rune. "Was that really necessary?"

"I think we both know it was, given what you're reading, darling." Rune gave the paperwork a pointed look. "John's nap will give you a chance to come up with a way to explain away *that*."

"I don't even remember taking samples, let alone sending them to John." Quickly lost in her own thoughts despite her distress over John moments before, Athena pushed her glasses up her nose and focused on the paperwork, murmuring absently, "I'm surprised I involved a relative stranger in this because I definitely see now why I might've wanted it kept offline." The corners of her mouth tugged down, and she tapped her pursed lips with her forefinger before rambling on. "Which implies I knew these results would be crazy."

Her brows shot up as she continued scanning the paperwork and essentially had a conversation with herself. "I would lose my colleagues' respect if this got out. They would think I falsified my samples somehow...had to have..."

"How so?" Quinn asked, just as curious as the rest of them by Athena's findings.

"For starters, the sample I took from the ash tree out front dates back further than pre-historic times. Past every extinction-level event on record." Athena shook her head. "Where the soil it grew in hasn't been here nearly as long."

"The tree is that old because it is part of a network of Yggdrasil's," Rune said, almost as if she expected Athena to know that by now. "And Yggdrasil's are not merely of this world but of the gods and all nine Norse worlds."

"Right...that...him," Athena said slowly, softly, clearly referring to Týr as she only partially paid attention and kept mulling over the sheets before her. "But even the samples I took from this house don't make sense, from the paint to the water."

"Is that because of you?" Athena pushed her glasses up her nose again and frowned at Rune. "Because of your magic's influence over this place?" Before Rune could respond, Athena fished a pencil out of her pocket, turned her nose back to her findings, and scratched notes while muttering away. "Actually, I was wrong. Some things *do* make sense. The dirt under the house's foundation matches the soil around the tree, so there's no magic there." She cocked her head and narrowed her eyes at her findings. "Yet the paint samples match no known compounds."

"Any more than magic does," Týr said, manifesting another ale before Rune did it for him, untrustworthy wench.

"True." Athena nodded and kept writing, rubbing her lips together in a distracting way that kept drawing his eye. A way that made him want to sample them more by the moment.

"So what were the results from the hearth?" Quinn wondered. "Or should I say the ashes on the hearth?"

"Um..." Athena kept leafing through the papers until she stopped and narrowed her eyes in disbelief. "That can't be right."

What she said next more than confirmed Týr had been correct when he said she would be leaving with him. However, he never could have imagined things wouldn't be nearly as simple as he'd hoped.

Chapter Three

"THIS JUST CAN'T be right," Athena repeated, staring at the results from the hearth's samples. "This is definitely volcanic ash, but it's not how it should be." She shook her head slowly, trying to make sense of it. "Something's off...different..."

She might seem entirely wrapped up in the unbelievable results she peered down at, yet she wasn't nearly as focused as she could be. Not because Rune made her friend John nod off with magical coffee, either, but because of the distracting Viking sitting across from her. Týr's steady gaze rarely left her, and she didn't need to look at him to know it. She could feel it, *him*, in a way that made her grow warmer and warmer.

Could he truly be taken with her and not one of her friends? That made no sense because it never happened. Men weren't typically attracted to her, and when she was with any of her Fire Anonymous friends, forget it. She faded into the background, and she was fine with that. Used to it.

Comfortable with it.

Now, here she was, the sole focus of a male dragon like Týr.

A man who was much more handsome than she'd initially thought with his rugged good looks and chiseled features. Of course, he still wasn't her type, as she preferred men who looked like John. At least slighter in build, to be sure. She wasn't as tall as her friends, either, so Týr was a bit of a giant next to her.

If all that wasn't enough, she had never embraced her inner dragon, let alone dated a male dragon because she knew better. Not only were they too fierce with more violent natures, but they breathed fire.

Beautiful, mesmerizing, *damning* fire.

"What's off about the results?" Quinn asked, pulling her from her private fascination with Týr and, of course, flames in general, as her friend crouched in front of the hearth and fingered the ashes left from the last fire. "I don't sense anything irregular here."

"Yet they are." Athena shook her head again. "My results show compounds that shouldn't be there. Ones I've never seen before. Possibly a type of wood despite presenting more like metal."

"Wood *and* metal?" Týr rumbled uneasily. He crouched beside Quinn and scooped up a handful of ashes, only to go perfectly still.

Terrifyingly still.

Seconds later, he seemed to figure something out because his mouth flattened into a hard, unresolved line, and his eyebrows slammed together. Suddenly furious and imposing as ever, he scowled and strode Athena's way in all his intimidating Far Too Tall glory, but Zoey blocked him.

"I might not look like much," Zoey snarled, baring just enough teeth to mean business, "but if you take one more step toward my friend with that look on your face, you won't like what I throw at you, Týr."

Like Athena, Zoey adored fire—at least half the time—and excelled at manipulating it if given half a chance.

"You destroyed it!" Týr accused Athena over Zoey's head. "Those ashes are from my shield, woman!"

When his sizzling blue dragon eyes flared at her, it felt like all the oxygen was sucked from the room, and she couldn't drag in air.

"Stop," she mouthed, putting a hand to her throat, gasping desperately because hers wasn't just an emotional response. She literally couldn't breathe. "Stay away."

"What are you *doing* to her?" Quinn cried, only for Athena to finally drag in a heavy gulp of air when Týr's dragon eyes returned to normal.

Still standing firmly between them, Zoey frowned from Týr to Athena. "Are you alright, hun?"

"I am," Athena managed, inhaling deeply as she set aside her papers.

Oddly, the weapons hanging around the room only she and Týr could see seemed more numerous than ever when she realized with sudden certainty he hadn't done that to her on purpose. More blades appeared on the walls by the moment. By the very second.

Like she was a magnet across time for the things he valued most.

"Týr didn't cause that...not really..." she went on, trying her best not to shy away from his angry look. "I have no idea what happened to your shield or why it might now be nothing but ashes. What I *do* know, however, and can't say why, is that it still exists somewhere, and we need to figure out what volcano those ashes came from because it's important somehow." A shiver ran through her. "*Really* important."

"What makes you say that?" Zoey asked, still keeping a wary eye on Týr. "Surely you have *some* inkling of why, Athena?"

27

Týr also seemed aware of his weapons appearing because his gaze traveled slowly around the room, and his brow lowered. "Whether she truly knows why or not, she says it because more of my weapons are manifesting here." He blinked in disbelief when it seemed he suddenly understood something even Athena hadn't figured out yet. "They're following her, *us*, because they mean to protect me." He seemed both awed and confused. "*She* means to protect me."

"Are you a Valkyrie like Keira?" Zoey asked Athena, astonished.

"I hope not, considering how much I hate violence." Athena swallowed hard, not just at the horrifying amount of savage weaponry surrounding them but by Týr's daunting realization.

She'd been astounded when Quinn told her that Keira, Athena's *best* friend, possessed the blood of a Valkyrie? A fabled warrior goddess sent by Odin? It would have seemed unbelievable before arriving here, but after seeing Ulrik and his Viking kin firsthand, then witnessing Týr's bizarrely manifested weapons only the two of them could see, it all seemed more and more plausible even to her left-brained way of thinking.

All but one thing, that is, because she hated violence.

Absolutely *had* to, for everyone's sake.

"I'm a scientist, not a fighter," she made clear to Týr despite more weapons continuing to appear as if summoned by her. "That's how I help humanity." She tapped her temple as though that could somehow make all this better. "With intellect and progress versus violence and dissent."

"Yet my weapons follow you," he said gruffly, seeming as unsettled by the idea as her yet, thankfully, no longer accusing her of destroying his shield. "And they represent protection, do they not?"

"They also represent death and destruction," Athena countered.

"Not a shield, though," Rune said softly, bringing the conversation back where Athena didn't want it. "A shield means nothing more than protection." The seer tilted her head in question. "Why do you think the ashes on the hearth are so important? If they possess elements from Týr's shield, could it be, like the shield itself, they protect Týr in some way?"

"I don't know," Athena said, confused when it seemed a memory hovered just out of reach. "Or *do* I?"

Flashes of her nightmare flickered in her mind's eye. A mountain. Trees. A vulnerable village. A man roaring. Or *was* it a man?

"I need to find that volcano," she murmured. "I need to..."

She trailed off when she swore the ashes on the fireplace moved. "Did you see that?"

"See what?" Quinn wondered when Athena drifted that way.

"I don't know." She shook her head. "Movement, I think."

Was there something under the ash? Something trying to break free?

"I need to see," she said softly, compelled, only to lose her breath when Týr grabbed her wrist before she could get any closer. Yet again, she gasped, struggling to draw in air before a tiny dragon burst from the ashes and staggered across the floor, clearly suffocating just like her.

"Help it," she gasped as the world grew dim, then flipped over when Týr scooped her into his arms. "Save it..."

After that, only bits and pieces came through. Darkness then dim light. A towering tree. A warm white glow. Cloying ash. A fresh burst of air. The scent of sea salt. Icy snowflakes against her cheeks. The chill of sea spray across her neck.

Then, the sizzling warmth of hard flesh.

She inhaled sharply, drawing in a male dragon's unique, spicy scent before her eyes shot open to complete darkness.

"It's okay," Týr rumbled against her ear from what seemed a great distance away, even though she knew she was in his arms. "Just give the tree a moment."

The tree? What was he talking about?

Seconds later, a dim glow filled the darkness, but she still couldn't make out anything. It was all a terrible blur.

Panicked, she croaked, "My glasses."

"They were lost, sweetie," Keira's welcome voice said. A comforting hand rested against her forehead. "Just give it a moment...give me and the tree just a few more moments..."

"I don't understand," she said hoarsely. "I don't..."

She trailed off when her surroundings became less and less blurry, and Keira's welcome face became clearer and clearer.

"Can you see me?" Keira asked gently as the golden light around her faded.

"I can," she whispered, touching where her glasses had once been.

She could see clearly without them.

Really, truly see.

Keira appeared every inch the beautiful Viking warrior now in her black leather attire. Small braids were interwoven in her long, curly, flaming red hair and her flawless bronzed skin glowed just as warmly as it ever did.

"Hey, there," Athena murmured, relieved to see her best friend alive and well.

"Hey," Keira said just as softly, smiling, clearly glad to see her in one piece, too.

Athena meant to say more, but her eyes drifted to the golden tree branches overhead, then locked with Týr's, and whatever she was going to say to Keira was lost to her. Once again, she found breathing impossible, but now it was for a different reason entirely. Gazing into his eyes at this proximity felt like having the wind knocked right out of her.

Like she had just made a groundbreaking discovery but much stronger.

That's when she realized she sat on his lap with his strong arms wrapped around her. When she understood the unusual sensation she felt wasn't just desire but his fear over what had happened to her.

Such intense fear, she knew he was every bit as shaken by it as her.

He was once again dressed like he had been when they first met in a brown leather tunic, pants, and heavy boots. Even his hair was the same. Fierce, just like the rest of him. Only now, he didn't frighten her. If anything, she once again wondered how she'd ever found him unattractive.

"What happened?" Her voice sounded choppy even to her own ears. "Where am I?"

The man who only days before had seemed like a monster was suddenly her savior. Her lifeline in a world of hazy dreams and Rune-induced tea delirium.

"You have arrived in what is known as the Dragon Lair," Týr said gruffly, clearly just as affected by her as she was by him. "As to what happened to you, I cannot say, but we will discuss it." His gaze flickered from Keira, who crouched in front of them, back to Athena, almost as if he hated to look away. "I sense it is of great importance."

31

"Here." Keira held a cup to Athena's mouth when she tried to talk but found her mouth too dry. Burnt feeling even. "Drink."

Grateful for the cool water the moment it slid down her throat, she sat forward, wrapped her hands around the cup, and gulped it down.

"How do you feel?" Keira asked after Athena closed her eyes and sighed with relief as the terrible parchedness faded.

"Better," she said, grateful to find her voice again. She opened her eyes and smiled only to yelp with fear when purple dragon eyes stared back at her from the darkness beyond the glow of the tree.

"What the!" She tried to scramble off Týr and flee the sinister gaze, but it was too late. Týr kept her in his arms and stood as if she weighed nothing.

"In the main cave, Åse," he barked over his shoulder, evidently talking to whoever possessed those purple dragon eyes as he carried Athena from a smaller cave into a far larger, more daunting one. "And in human form."

"Is she so easily frightened then?" a sultry feminine voice answered from behind them. "Because such weakness will bode ill for your cock."

His *what*? Good God.

"Åse," Keira chastised. "Enough."

"I agree," came a masculine voice she recognized.

"Is that Ulrik?" Athena asked.

"King Ulrik," the crass feminine voice corrected, speaking in a foreign language she somehow understood. "King above all kings, so address him correctly, *svak en*."

"I'm not a weak one," Athena murmured despite feeling so physically drained. "At least not mentally."

The woman mumbled in disagreement, but Keira snapped something at her Athena didn't quite catch, and she went silent.

"Don't lay me down there," she murmured, sensing that Týr meant to lay her in a bed. "I want to sit up." When he hesitated and slowed, she made herself clear. "Please. I've been in bed for days. Let me sit with all of you and try to understand what's happening. Understand...where I am..."

Yet somehow, she already knew, and Týr confirmed it when he sat her in front of a sizeable fire in the center of the cave and told her she'd traveled back to his time.

Back to tenth century Norway.

She took in the massive cave adorned with even more weapons than the twenty-first-century living room she'd just left. A scary yet somehow beautiful and interesting place she could see so clearly now in a strange sort of way. Things had a sparkle about them that hadn't been there before. Dark corners seemed to lighten more by the moment.

Keira swung a chair close and sat beside Athena, her voice still gentle and her worry evident. "How are you feeling now?" Her friend's touch was blissfully cool against her chin as she steered Athena's gaze to her when she didn't respond right away. "Athena, are you with me?"

Unable to find her tongue the first time, she tried again and managed a soft, "I am."

"Good, because you'll be coming out of shock soon, and things will become even more overwhelming. My magic and that of the Yggdrasil helped you some, but not entirely." She held a cup out to Athena. "So, will you trust me and drink something that isn't quite water?"

"As long as it isn't alcohol," she said. "You know I can't handle that stuff anymore."

"I know," Keira replied. "This is something different. It'll soothe you and help you transition a little better."

"Are you sure?"

"I am."

She narrowed her eyes. "It's not like Rune's tea, is it?"

The corner of Keira's mouth inched up, and she shook her head. "Definitely not."

"Alright then." She nodded, sipped the warm, somewhat sweet liquid, and what a difference it made almost immediately.

"What *is* this?" she whispered in awe as strength filled her, and everything seemed to level out.

"A concoction I once made for Keira when she needed it most," a deep voice said before she realized Ulrik stood nearby, watching her with a kindness and compassion she would have never expected from a tenth-century Viking dragon king. "One meant to soothe your inner dragon."

"I see," she said even though she didn't because she'd had so little contact with her inner beast out of necessity, if nothing else. "Thanks."

She tried to say hello and smile at Ulrik, meant to congratulate him and Keira on finding love against the odds, but she couldn't seem to find the words. Instead, she felt a terrible sense of trepidation that only abated when she located Týr sitting in a subliminally throne-like chair a ways off. Distanced from them, somehow.

Distanced from her.

Their eyes connected in a moment that felt disconnected and dangerous yet terribly familiar before she dragged her gaze away and looked at Keira again. "What happened? The last thing I remember, I couldn't breathe, then I was choking, then..." Remembering the ash-covered baby dragon, she shook her head and shivered. "Then I saw it..."

"And it saw you," Keira said softly. "That's when things became truly difficult." She gently turned Athena's arm over and showed her something that made her blood run cold. "More difficult than you might be ready for."

Chapter Four

TÝR HAD BATTLED thousands of warriors. Ended too many lives to count and without a shred of guilt if it meant keeping his people safe. Ulrik's and Rafe's people safe. Yet now, for no reason that he understood, one life meant more than all the rest.

One life packaged in a small, helpless twenty-first-century female who was so detached from her dragon it was shameful. A woman who earned his devotion for no other reason than how he felt the first time he gazed into her eyes without her glasses.

For the undeniable impact her brilliant blue dragon eyes had on him.

Or so he told himself, despite suspecting it had happened even sooner. A connection that grew rapidly, then exploded when he saw what staggered out of the hearth's ashes back at the Maine chalet.

"What *is* this?" Athena gasped, staring down with horror at the shadowy tattoo of a small dragon on her inner arm. "How did..." Fortunately, as she blinked and shook her head, Ulrik's concoction eased her panic, and she took a long, deep, calming breath before continuing. "What happened?" She looked from Keira to Týr. "Tell me."

Týr had known she was beautiful when he'd watched her sleep the past two nights but hadn't been fully prepared for just how stunning she would be when her glasses were gone and her glorious eyes were open. Big sapphire eyes that teetered between human and dragon. A shade of blue so magnificent they made a crystal-clear sea and pure sunlit sky pale in comparison. A hue so magnetic they could pull a man into a thick, alluring web she had no idea she possessed.

"Tell me what happened, Týr," Athena repeated, drawing him back to the here and now.

How best to phrase it? The way he had seen it, he supposed.

Better yet, how he'd *felt* it.

"From what I could tell, you summoned a spirit of sorts," he said. "A female dragon born of ashes."

"Born of ashes?" Athena shook her head. "I don't understand."

"Nor do I." He narrowed his eyes at Åse, warning her to behave as she kept to the shadows in human form. "What I do know is you felt that tiny dragon's suffering." Still seeing it so clearly, *feeling* it so intensely, he inhaled deeply before continuing. "She had been burned beyond repair...beyond recognition..." He manifested a horn of ale but didn't gulp it down like he wanted to out of respect for the moment. "She could pull air into her lungs no more than you as she staggered toward you."

"Then?" Athena prompted softly when he paused, still trying to understand what he'd witnessed.

When he continued to hesitate, Keira urged him to go on.

"Then you dropped to your knees despite my holding your wrist, held out your hand to the little dragon, and she leapt—" his gaze dropped to Athena's wrist where the tattoo now rested— "into you as far as I could tell."

"*Into* me?" Athena exclaimed. She frowned and shook her head, unsettled. "I don't understand. What does that mean? Did it possess me somehow?"

"I think if it did, you would know." Ulrik crouched in front of Athena and gestured at her arm. "Might I take a closer look?"

Týr frowned at the strange sensation that rolled through him when she offered her arm, and Ulrik ran his fingers over the tattoo. What was this uncomfortable feeling?

"*That would be jealousy, mate,*" Åse said telepathically, melting out of the darkness. She rested her hip against him where he sat in his chair a ways from Athena, keeping his distance until he better understood his overwhelming draw to her.

"*And I cannot see why you are jealous,*" Åse went on, her disapproval obvious. "*I sense your svak en cannot even fight. That she loathes everything about it, which means she will likely keep her thighs shut to you.*" She snorted. "*I do not think she could handle your cock anyway. She is far too—*"

"What?" Athena muttered under her breath. Surprisingly enough, not only was she following their telepathic conversation, but her dragon eyes flared when they narrowed on Åse. "Naïve? Detached from my inner dragon?"

Clearly pleased to see a little fire in her, Åse didn't hold back. "I was going to say virginal."

"Åse," Keira exclaimed, shooting her a look. "*Enough.*"

Týr tensed at Åse's revelation. Athena was *virginal*? How had he not sensed that? As it was, he'd been shocked his cock behaved when she was on his lap, given how appealing he had found her rounded bottom. Now he wondered...was his inner beast trying not to frighten her? Overwhelm her? He couldn't imagine. Then again, he had never met a woman, let alone a female dragon still virginal at her age.

It made her a rare treasure in more ways than one.

Athena's jaw dropped at Åse's untimely revelation, then snapped shut. Her cheeks flamed pink, and she looked anywhere but at him.

"I can't sense anything," Ulrik said, breaking the uncomfortable moment as he released her arm. "Whatever magic resides in your tattoo, Athena, it's different than anything I've encountered before."

Alarming, considering Ulrik was the most powerful dragon ever to exist.

"What about Rafe?" Keira also touched the tattoo but shook her head, clearly feeling nothing. "Isn't this sort of thing right up his alley?"

"It is." Ulrik stood and considered Athena. "I sense you're eager to find the mountain with the right ash and perhaps Týr's shield, but you need food and rest first. My brew will help ease your dragon into its new environment, but whatever happened to you when this tattoo formed sapped more energy than you realize." He shot Åse a look before introducing them properly. "Forgive my second-in-command's behavior. She will no longer be so rude if she hopes to continue on with us in the morning."

"Of course, my King." Åse casually and perhaps a tad possessively rested her hand on Týr's shoulder and nodded once, her tone cordial enough when she looked at Athena. "Forgive me, Athena. It seems I am more protective of my mate than I realized."

"Mate?" He sensed Athena's heart rate increase as she looked from Týr to Åse. "I didn't realize." She swallowed and seemed to gather herself. "Nice to meet you, Åse."

"Åse is my friend," he corrected, for some reason needing Athena to understand that where he'd never much cared what other women he'd lain with thought of his longstanding arrangement with Åse. Rather than continue the conversation, he gestured at one of his people to see food and drink brought out. "Let us dine, then rest." He looked at Åse. "See that the others stay away for the night while Athena adjusts to her surroundings."

"Of course." Obviously unable to help herself, Åse perked a brow. "Should I visit your bed later, *friend*? Perhaps now Athena is here, your cock will work again."

He sighed and scowled when Åse didn't bother waiting for an answer but winked at Athena and sauntered off.

"If you think you'll be okay without me, Athena, I could really use some rest." Keira yawned and rested her hand on her stomach. "I think Valkyrie babies zap their mom's strength more than most."

"What?" Athena's eyes widened on Keira's mid-drift. "No way! *Really?*"

Keira smiled. "Really."

"Oh, *wow*." Athena embraced her and then grinned from Ulrik to Keira. "Congratulations, you two." She squeezed Keira's hand. "Of course, go get some rest. I'll be fine."

"Are you sure?" Keira glanced from Týr to her. "Because I was hoping to drag Ulrik along with me."

Which would leave the two of them alone.

That evidently didn't bother Athena as much as it would have hours ago because something had shifted between them when the Yggdrasil brought her here.

Something that had everything to do with their inner beasts.

"I'm sure I'll be fine without you two." Athena shooed Keira along. "Off you go. Sleep well."

41

Týr would have thought nothing of Ulrik joining Keira if he hadn't sensed his cousin's fear, which chilled him.

"Tell me what plagues our females is not affecting Keira as well," he said to his brethren on a telepathic link that should have been theirs alone.

"It's not," Keira assured, clearly so connected to Ulrik now there was no way around her catching their internal conversations. *"So don't worry."*

"We do not know that with any certainty," Ulrik said, his concern obvious.

"Yes, we do." Keira continued talking, but the conversation faded from Týr's mind, no doubt Keira's way of letting him know this was between her and her husband.

"Is everything alright?" Athena asked tentatively after they left. She glanced from the tunnel Keira and Ulrik had just vanished down to Týr. "You look worried."

"Everything's fine," he said, hoping he was right.

"You're lying," Athena said softly. He sensed her mild discomfort at being left alone with him, but she pressed on. "I'm not sure how I know that, but you are."

She knew it because their dragons were connecting, and he had no idea what to make of it. How he was supposed to feel. However, he knew Athena should be told the truth now she had traveled back in time and was so clearly a part of all this.

So he abandoned his throne, rested a small table between them for food, then sat down with her and explained what was happening to their women. How they were growing weaker and losing their magic.

"Not all of them, but many," he said in closing, pained by what was happening. "Including our matriarchs."

"I'm so sorry to hear that." Worried, Athena's gaze flickered from Keira's tunnel to Týr. "And you think that might be happening to Keira too? That fast?"

"I couldn't say but pray not because it wouldn't be good for anyone but most of all my king." He could not even fathom it. "From what I've heard and feel inside Ulrik now, there is no greater pain than a dragon's mate growing ill. Worse still, his offspring."

"I can't even imagine," she replied, her thoughts much like his from what he caught of them. She had not experienced love, so she could not truly empathize.

"Have your women suffered any other symptoms?" Athena wondered, absently going to push up glasses that were no longer there. "Or just those two things?"

"Just symptoms that go along with weakening," he said. "Lack of appetite. Listlessness." He thought about it. "Sadness and exhaustion."

"When did it start?" She tilted her head in question. "Was something going on at the time? A change in the weather or your food supply? With your livestock or grains? Perhaps with your drinking water?"

"No." He appreciated her concern because it was genuine. More than that, it was a concern she need not feel, given she had been thrust into all this without any choice. "As far as we know, nothing changed, so we are of the mind either the gods willed it or perhaps an unseen enemy."

"That would be a pretty powerful enemy, wouldn't it?" Her delicate eyebrows edged together. "Would a dragon be capable of that?"

"Normally, I would say no, but I fear as time has gone on and unrest grows between our kingdoms, it becomes more difficult to know what others are truly capable of." He swigged his ale and sighed. "Evil can sprout up anywhere and remain unseen if it wishes."

"So you think it might be a dragon?"

"I think anything is possible, and it would be foolish to assume otherwise."

"I agree." She sipped her brew and considered him. "Do you think this unseen enemy lives within your own allied kingdoms? Perhaps even a family member?

"You mean Zane." He could only assume Rune or one of her friends had caught her up on some things but not others because she hadn't known about Keira's pregnancy. Yet she clearly knew that, on Ulrik and Keira's adventure, they learned there was an enemy amidst them. Or at least someone with a nefarious plan Týr guessed was to usurp Ulrik and rule over all of Norway.

"Zane seems the most likely suspect from what I've heard." She paused for a moment, hesitant, before she went on. "Do you think I'll be able to go to the Realm? Not the Keep, I don't think, but the Realm sounds like it would be a scientist's dream. Your gods made it, right? Created it from elements I'm sure are just as foreign as what was in those ashes back home?"

Zane ruled over the Keep these days, and the Keep was in the Realm.

"Níðhöggr created the Realm many generations ago," he replied. "He was one of the most powerful dragons ever born to our homeworld, Múspellsheimr, so, *ja*, I think it would be full of foreign elements." He stilled when he caught something and narrowed his eyes. "You don't want to go there just for unknown elements, though, do you?"

"Of course I do." Despite her curiosity, there was a nervous edge to her voice when she glanced at the cave's shadows and eyed a dragon or two brave enough to defy Åse and watch Athena from the darkness. "Why else would I want to go there?"

He tried to ignore that strange sensation when it surged again. Had Åse been right? Was he experiencing jealousy of all things?

"I could not say why else you would want to go…" he began before it came to him. It wasn't fellow males she was interested in but what they were capable of. "You crave their fire."

"Whose fire?" she asked a little too innocently, burying her question in another sip.

"You must have been told the Realm is home to the bulk of Ancients and Múspellsheimr dragons," he surmised. "Which gives you not just fire but flames from dragons of another world."

"It would be something to see," she admitted. A flash of excitement twinkled in her eyes before she cleared her throat and corrected herself. "What I mean to say is I would love to study them to see if their fire burns differently than normal fire, be it from Earthly dragons or, say, a volcano."

"Keira told me about the support group where you two first met." He eyed her as he downed his ale, wondering how concerned he should be. "Should I assume you are addicted to fire rather than put off by it?"

"I am…addicted, that is." She set her cup down on the table and twirled it methodically as though trying to fight a craving at that very moment. "But I manage it by remaining as close to it as possible. By studying volcanoes and running experiments, I can avoid needing it elsewhere."

"So you are…what is the twenty-first-century word?" He thought about it. "A pyromaniac?"

"That's what they say." She sighed and twirled her cup in the opposite direction. "Only ten times worse because I'm half dragon. So the damage I could inflict if I give in to my addiction, or become

45

unhinged as we call it, could very well be worldwide and substantial."

"I see." How interesting and more than a little daunting. Yet somehow, he found it alluring. Perhaps because one would never guess it by looking at her. Never suspect she had such a fiery passion burning within her, even if it was destructive. "Hence your aversion to violence."

"To say the least," she said. "It's at the root of so many things that have the potential to end in fire. Just look at the violence of battles and wars for example, no matter what century they take place in. Always a burning building. A town razed. Always fire and destruction. Therefore, I have to hate it above all else for its ability to satisfy my fire cravings."

"And you manage those cravings by subjecting yourself to fire for a living," he marveled, not quite understanding. "I would think that would do the opposite."

"Yet it doesn't." She shook her head. "By focusing on volcanoes and everything they're capable of, including fire, I can keep my dragonly urges at bay. It's hard to explain, but it works."

"Because volcanoes fascinate not just your human half but your inner dragon," he murmured, seeing it clearly enough. More so, feeling it within her.

"Yes," she said softly. Her eyes lingered on his in a way she would have been incapable of before. "That's right."

"And now here you are amid more temptation than you've ever been subjected to." His dragons were smart enough to skulk away when he glared into the darkness. "Not to mention you are a virgin."

"That's really none of your business." She frowned into her cup, without a doubt wishing there was more, and with good reason because it was loosening her inner beast considerably.

"And it definitely wasn't Åse's place to say," Athena went on. "What's her problem anyway?" She turned her frown his way. "She realizes you and I aren't...whatever she might think, right? She understands that I'm no threat to you two?"

"Not to Åse, no," he agreed. "But you're a very big threat to me."

Then, because it was time that she understood what she was in for, he made things perfectly clear.

-Her Viking Dragon Warrior-

Chapter Five

ATHENA COULD NOT have heard Týr correctly. Prayed she hadn't.

"So you're telling me—" she said warily after the sensual woman who gazed at Týr the whole time she set food down on the table sauntered off— "that I'm going to be a walking target here because I'm...a virgin?"

She felt foolish and more than a little embarrassed having this conversation with a relative stranger, but she understood why Týr felt the need to share what she could expect. And it wasn't good.

In fact, it was terrifying.

"In this day and age, because our females are weakening and there are less of them being born in general," he replied, reiterating what he had just said, "fertile, strong female dragons are in high demand." He did away with his horn and manifested ale in a cup. "Virgin females are sought after every bit as much as females in heat."

"And why is that again?" Because, as far as she knew, virgin dragons were no more fertile than any other female dragon.

"Beyond obvious reasons," he replied, showing no signs of amusement where a modern-day guy might, "in this era, a virgin female tends to commit fully to the male who takes her first. A means, I imagine, to find protection against other males as time goes on." He shrugged. "This, in turn, gives males a higher chance of creating offspring and keeping their lineage going."

"Dear Lord, that sounds terribly medieval," she said, surprised when her cup refilled itself with Ulrik's brew. Not that she was complaining because it really was working wonders.

"My king sees to his people," Týr said, noting the cup as he urged her to eat from a variety of scrumptious-smelling meats, cheeses, and breads. "And you are his people as long as you are here."

"Yet you're clearly in charge at this location," she commented, fully aware that the male dragons lurking nearby earlier had skulked off after he'd cast them a dark look. "So that makes you what?"

"Some call me an earl. Others refer to me as a lesser king." He put a variety of meats on her wooden plate when she made no move to eat. "Either way, unlike my more traitorous kin lately, I only serve and answer to my cousin and friend, King Ulrik. He is king above kings and should be honored as such."

The more comfortable she became in her own skin because that was the only way to describe what Ulrik's brew did for her, the more questions she had. How much had the Yggdrasil really affected her when she traveled back in time? Would her eyesight go again? Why was she truly here? What was she supposed to accomplish? And why, again, was she a threat to Týr because of her virginity? Yet one question kept rising above all others.

Were Týr and Åse together or not?

She could say without hesitation that she didn't like Åse in the least. The stunning woman with black braids tied back in a high ponytail and leather clothing that hugged her perfect figure far too tightly was nothing less than a bully.

"Now is not the time to keep questions to yourself," Týr said around a mouthful of meat. "You have traveled back to a dangerous time in history, made more dangerous still because we are warring, desperate dragons, so speak your mind. Ask your questions so you might be armed with knowledge if not a weapon."

She could admit she was surprised by Týr as a whole. When she'd first laid eyes on him, she had thought him an uneducated brute full of battle lust, but he was proving to be more under all those muscles. Proving he wasn't only intelligent and protective but also perceptive, humble, loyal, and forthright.

He was also proving that he followed her thoughts a little too easily.

Regardless, he was right, so she asked away as she ate, only to receive concise, decisive answers. As it had for Keira, the Yggdrasil helped her transition along with Ulrik's brew. Helped her begin merging with her dragon in an essential way. He had no idea if her eyesight would worsen again, but it didn't matter because they could manifest glasses for her.

He couldn't say what her true purpose was here, only that it no doubt had to do with a volcano and most certainly better have to do with getting his shield back. Either way, he would stand by her side and defend her if for no other reason than she was likely here to help his people.

"As to Åse," he said, sipping his ale, "she worries that your virginity is going to put me in harm's way, and she's right because I will defend it with my life if necessary. Unlike many from my era and those who choose to ignore the lessons of our upbringing, I was raised by a twenty-first-century mother who time traveled, so I understand your body is yours to give to a man, not his to take."

Another woman from the future? Seriously? But that was beside the point at the moment. Just when she thought she couldn't be more impressed, Týr once again proved he was so much more than a mere warrior.

"As to Åse and me," he rambled on, giving her honesty that she both appreciated and was taken aback by, "she and I have long shared a bed, but not exclusively. She has a woman at the Fortress she likes to frequent, and I generally need more than even she can offer."

"I see." Although she didn't. "So you..." *What? Are way too sexual? Addicted to it, even?* "Need a lot of..." *For goodness sake, just say it, Athena.* "Sex?"

"*Ja*," he confirmed without hesitation and without any sign of flirtation. If anything, he was clinical about it, and with good reason, it seemed.

"Until you first connected with me, I suffered from mood swings of a sort due to my inner Helheim." He polished off the last of his food and downed his ale in two long swallows. "Laying with a woman was the only way to keep my spirits up. To that end, Åse agreed when we were younger that she would see to my needs when she could." He nodded once as if merely talking about a good buddy. "She has been a very good friend since. The best."

Some might interpret that as Åse was great in bed, which Athena suspected was true based on her confident attitude, but she was fairly certain Týr didn't mean it that way. In his eyes, Åse satisfied his physical needs and, in turn, his mood and mind, so she was simply a good friend who looked after his wellbeing.

"I'm surprised it never turned into anything more," she said before she could stop herself, but in truth, she was curious and, again, more comfortable by the moment, thanks to Ulrik's brew. It was so nice to drink something that made her feel good without addling her mind or making her crave fire.

Týr frowned in confusion at him and Åse becoming something more. "What do you mean, more?"

Wow. Really? And here she thought she was clueless about this topic.

"As in love," she prompted. "That emotion that sometimes goes hand in hand with sex."

"I have seen it," he admitted as if it were as foreign to him as it was her. "Between my parents and aunts and uncles." He shook his head and manifested another ale. "But it's not something I've ever felt or needed. If anything, it makes people, dragons especially, far too vulnerable."

"I imagine you're right." She had often heard of people, especially dragons, doing stupid things because of love.

"So you've been better since we met?" she asked once again before she could stop herself. "Your inner Helheim has calmed down?" Before he could reply, she rambled on, too curious for her own good. "What does that mean, exactly? What is your *inner Helheim?*"

"Something to be discussed on the morrow," he said, noting the time and ignoring his newly manifested ale. "Ulrik will want to get to the Stronghold before the storm comes, so we must be up early."

Truth be told, she was shocked hours had gone by since they began talking. Surprised she had enjoyed their conversation and looked forward to more. Almost as if Ulrik's brew knew Týr wanted her to rest, exhaustion washed over her, and she yawned.

Where hours before, she would have been terrified when Týr led her down a torch-lit tunnel different than the one Keira had gone down earlier, now she wasn't scared in the least. Rather, she felt safe with Týr, knowing he wouldn't try anything. Or so she thought until he led her into a huge seaside cave with a sizeable fur-clad bed.

"This is your lair," she managed hoarsely, inhaling without meaning to. She stopped short when she felt him everywhere in a way she'd never felt another. It was strange and primal, and she didn't trust it.

"It is." He doused the torches on either side of the bed with a chant and gestured that way. "Go sleep. I will watch over you."

Negative. Not a good idea. "Watch over me?"

"*Ja.*" He gestured at the bed again, then at a chair in the far corner that overlooked both entrances. "I will sit there and watch over you lest anyone try to take advantage of your virginity."

"Oh, marvelous," she muttered under her breath, still not nearly as frightened as she should be. "And what are the odds of that, exactly? Statistically speaking, of course?"

"Zero percent if I watch over you," he replied without batting a lash. "One hundred percent if I do not."

Despite that being a horrifying statistic, she couldn't help a small smile because he did, indeed, clearly have a twenty-first-century mother and because something about her big bad Viking laying out stats so matter-of-factly was unexpected.

Yet again, eased by him, by his very presence, trusting him when some might say she shouldn't quite yet, she nodded and relented. "Okay."

Keeping on everything but her shoes, she was grateful for his plush furs when she crawled into bed because it was cold and gusty. Nonetheless, she could admit she liked it as she cozied down and inhaled his spicy pine scent. It reminded her of a memory that, once more, seemed just out of reach.

"You should try to sleep," she said into his mind as she watched him sit and eye both entrances like a hawk. Better yet, like a dragon people seriously didn't want to mess with. *"You can't sit up all night."*

"I can and I will," he rumbled back telepathically, invoking all sorts of unusual feelings. Erotic sensations that were foreign to her, from a warm, blossoming pleasure between her thighs to a heaviness in her breasts.

"Because of my inner Helheim, a sort of biological godliness I inherited from Goddess Hel, I am half of the land of the dead, so I don't need to sleep as much as others," he continued. *"So rest easy, Athena."*

Right. Helheim. Had he said Goddess *Hel?* But somehow, that made sense and suited him being a vicious warrior she was certain had escorted too many to count to their death via his blade. To Helheim itself. And that should terrify her. Make him abhorrent.

But somehow it didn't.

Rather, he seemed a dark angel as she grew more sleepy and tried to focus on him. So he was half what? Undead? That didn't seem right when he was so very much alive. So incredibly viral and masculine and...

That was the last thought she had before sunlight washed over her the next morning, and she woke to find a dark devil staring down at her.

"Are you awake then, *svak en?*" Åse grunted, with her arms crossed over her chest. "Or did you intend to sleep away as my mate readies a ship for you when you should be helping? When you *should* be pulling your weight in exchange for his protection?"

"I am *not* a weak one," she muttered in response to the damnable nickname Åse had given her. She frowned when she realized Týr was gone, and she was alone with the obstinate Viking woman.

"You are weak until you prove otherwise." Åse eyed her with dismay when Athena sat up and yawned. "I cannot understand what his cock sees in you, but we will work toward helping it along even more."

Before Athena could respond to that ridiculous assessment, Åse gestured at a pool of water in the corner. "Bathe, then I will dress you because you cannot remain here in those dreadful clothes."

"What's the matter with my clothes?" She frowned at Åse and pulled her blazer tighter around her chest as she stood. "They're perfectly acceptable."

"They are pointless." Åse nudged her toward the water. "Wash the stink of other women off of you, then I will help you make sex with Týr better."

"The stink of other women?" she managed, trudging along because, quite frankly, Åse was a little scary with the endless weapons strapped to her fit body. "And I'm sorry, but I'm not having sex with Týr. Even if I did, you would be the last one I would want help from with that."

"*Ja*, the stink of other women in his bed," Åse replied, answering her first question. "He does not know better than to wash them away when he has a virgin present." She kept nudging Athena along. "He desires you already, but that will not be enough if you do not feel desirable in return." She gestured flippantly from Athena's clothes to the water. "Now undress and bathe so I can do my best to fix you."

When Athena hesitated, Åse rested her hand on the dagger sheathed at her waist and perked her brows.

"I don't like you," Athena made clear, far more honest than she would have been even yesterday, thanks to whatever this place was doing to her.

"Any more than I like you," Åse replied just as bluntly.

"You realize you're a bully, right?" Athena grumbled, undressing. She would know because she'd dealt with her fair share during childhood. "A really mean one, at that."

"And you are weak and unworthy of my friend," Åse countered, scowling at her as she made her way into surprisingly warm water. "You will be the death of him if you do not learn how to protect yourself because he will like your body very much and continue to want you. Even worse, be vulnerable because he is distracted by you."

Like her body? *Please.* She might be closeted and even naïve at times, but she wasn't stupid. Men didn't desire her body. Yet when she glanced back, it was to find Åse turned away with her arms crossed over her chest again. She nearly asked why when she suddenly understood, most likely because of her connection with Týr and, in turn, Åse.

The Viking woman found her desirable. Because of that and out of respect to Týr and her own girlfriend, Åse would no longer watch Athena until she was dressed. As it turned out, that was mere minutes after she bathed and walked out, only for Åse to chant her into a whole new outfit.

"Absolutely not." She shook her head. "Absolutely *never* going to happen."

Or so she thought until Åse flicked her wrist, and the matter was taken out of her hands with results she never would have expected.

Chapter Six

"**Y**OU SHOULD HAVE assisted Athena in dressing appropriately for this era," Týr said to Keira as they readied the boat alongside Ulrik. "Åse cannot be trusted."

"Yet you placed your trust in her when you agreed to have her wake Athena," Keira reminded, clearly unconcerned. "We all know this needs to happen. Whatever might come of you and Athena, she's here, and your dragons are connecting. That means you're going to need your best friend more than ever." She gave Týr a pointed look. "And don't tell me Åse doesn't rank just a tad higher than everyone else in your life because we both know you'd be lying."

"She does not rank higher than Ulrik or Rafe," he denied, though she did, but not by much. "If she did, she would be my second-in-command instead of Ulrik's."

"And she would have been had you allowed it." Ulrik grinned. "If I recall correctly, you wanted the best warrior you knew defending your king and leading his armies."

That was true. He had. Glad to see Ulrik happy when he rarely had been dealing with warring kingdoms over the years, he met his grin. Hoped it meant that Keira's exhaustion the night before was nothing more than pregnancy.

"Wanting the best warrior defending Ulrik *does* sound like something you would want, Týr," Keira agreed, about to go on when her gaze locked on something over his shoulder, and her jaw dropped. "Holy *shit*."

He couldn't agree more when he turned and locked eyes on Athena.

Hell, if having the twenty-first-century woman in his bed last night without touching her hadn't been torture enough, Åse had, without a doubt, made matters ten times worse.

How else could it be when she'd ripped away Athena's overly conservative attire and turned her into an alluring goddess? Because she was most certainly that, wearing an outfit similar to Åse's but somehow sensually lethal on Athena. Dressed from head to toe in plush black leather that hugged her sinfully curvy body, from her full breasts to her lush hips, she had gone from beautiful to stunning. From unapproachable to a seductress who would be his undoing, and his cock made that obvious before he could take another breath.

"Ah, *there* it is," Åse exclaimed, pointing out his erection with a smile as she rolled her eyes at Athena and sauntered their way, throwing over her shoulder, "You're welcome."

Meanwhile, clearly transported here within moments of being dressed, Athena looked from her outfit to his arousal in such a baffled way he might have found it amusing if he didn't feel her mortification. It was hard to know if it was because of her outfit or his erection, but it didn't matter. He chanted her into a black fur cloak and willed his arousal away with everything in him as he leapt off the ship and headed Athena's way in case she passed out again.

"Are you alright, Athena?" He closed the distance quickly. "Do you feel ill again?"

Surprisingly, a part of him feared she might be suffering from the illness affecting so many females here. That she may be in the same peril.

"I'm fine," she managed, more than a little winded as she looked anywhere but at him, and her cheeks flamed pink. "Just embarrassed on a few fronts."

"As I said last night, you need not fear my cock." It took everything in him not to pull her into his arms and hold her until her racing heart calmed. "It will not go near you without your consent."

Athena bit her lower lip and chuckled a little before her gaze finally found his face, and she chuckled again. "You really do say the strangest things, but...thank you for that."

Unsure how to respond, he nodded and did his best to remember the things his mother had taught him growing up. Formalities he'd never bothered with until now because he hadn't needed to. The women that had come and gone from his bed over the years did not require nor want such niceties.

"You look..." *Exquisite? Sinfully gorgeous?* No, too much too soon. "Very nice."

Åse mumbled something about her looking far better than very nice from the boat, but he ignored her. Instead, he focused on the rest of Athena, which was no hard task. Her lush little body might be hidden under the fur cloak now, but her face was never more lovely, with her hair weaved back in a myriad of thick, dark braids. Her blue eyes were more brilliant than ever against her soft, creamy skin, and she appeared more rested today, her vibrancy impossible to look away from.

"Thank you, Týr," she replied softly. Her cheeks only grew rosier. "That's sweet of you."

Sweet? When he frowned at the word, Åse echoed in the background that it was a compliment, however inaccurate because Viking dragon warriors were only ever the opposite of sweet.

"Come on, my friend." Keira grabbed Athena's hand and pulled her toward the boat. She winked at Týr over her shoulder that all was well and continued talking to Athena. "Your Viking makeover, which is really gorgeous, by the way, deserves a proper Viking ship to go with it, so let's get you out on the water."

"Really?" Athena took in the roiling black clouds outside the sizeable cave harbor. "Are you sure? It seems like that storm Ulrik was worried about might—"

"Still be on its way?" Keira leapt into the ship and helped Athena down. "It is, but not quite yet. These guys know their way around, so no worries. They wouldn't take us out if it was too dangerous."

Týr bit back amusement, considering they had done just that the first time they brought Keira out. Then again, Keira wasn't Athena, and he sensed that more by the moment. Some might think it was because Athena wouldn't like the rush of a good storm, but it was the opposite.

She might like it a bit too much.

Ulrik nodded in acknowledgment of his thoughts before Týr hopped into the boat. If Athena was subjected to a thrill on the high seas that involved lightning, she might very well guide it to strike the ship, so it ignited in fire. If that happened, there was no telling how far Athena would take it just to experience the rush flames could give her.

62

"Surely not," Åse said into his mind, sensing it as well. *"She would try to end us all?"*

"I would," Athena confirmed, surprising him with how easily she was able to listen in on his and Åse's conversation. "But it wouldn't be anything personal."

Týr could tell by how Åse eyed Athena she wasn't quite sure what to make of that. One part of her worried about keeping the others safe, whereas the other was impressed Athena had that sort of confidence. Or at least that's the way she saw it.

He, however, grew warier by the moment because of Athena's addiction. How harmful it might be to her because destruction in these parts meant retribution. If she hurt someone with flames, especially King Ulrik, the wrath of several kingdoms would come down on her, including, unfortunately, his own.

And that did not sit well at all.

Would he be capable of harming Athena if he had to? If given no other choice? Somehow, he didn't think so. In fact, deep down, he knew his inner dragon would never allow it. Therefore, her addiction was truly alarming and perhaps even useful to their enemies if they caught wind of it.

When his eyes connected with Athena's and her pupils flared, he knew she followed his thoughts and was fully aware of the danger she could put herself in. More so, she realized the danger she had put him in, not just with her virginity but with her addiction.

"We will remain close to the shore as we travel north," he said, joining Athena at the bow as the wind caught the sail and they lurched forward. "Far enough away from the incoming storm so there will be no risk."

"Okay." Athena seemed both caught by the experience of being on a Viking boat for the first time and wariness over the encroaching weather. "I don't usually have issues with lightning storms back home, but something tells me that might not be the case here, and I have no idea why."

"Perhaps because your dragon is becoming less repressed."

Athena looked at him with alarm. "I thought it was only becoming more transitioned to this place?" Her eyes widened, and she shook her head. "I've been keeping it repressed my whole life for a reason." She pointed at the weather. "That and anything else that would tempt it."

He felt her fear as if it were his own but kept it from her the best he could because panicking would do her no good. She must face this head-on with a level mind. "Then we must discover a way to overcome your addiction because I don't think your inner beast will be held back by your human half much longer."

"I'm afraid you might be right," Athena murmured, rubbing her tattoo absently. "It's sensing way too many of its kind here." She surprised him yet again when she went on. "And in the vein of transparency, because I'd rather understand something than avoid it given the circumstances, it seems—" she cleared her throat— "it's more aware of you in particular."

Not that she had to tell him because his inner beast sensed it, he was grateful she felt comfortable enough to admit they were connecting.

"I don't entirely understand what that means." She pulled her cloak tighter against the biting wind, even though he sensed her skin warming at his proximity.

"I think you do." He steadied her against him when the boat hit a wave, and she teetered a little. "I think you knew the moment you crawled into my bed last night and inhaled my scent."

"I didn't...there wasn't..." She blinked several times, and her cheeks flamed redder still. "What I mean to say is..."

"She did catch your scent, but it wasn't as tempting as it might have been with so many other female scents there," Åse said bluntly, joining them as if it were her place to oversee whatever developed between them. "Her human half might not have caught it, but I suspect her dragon did."

"God, you just don't quit, do you?" Athena muttered, clearly embarrassed. "I didn't smell anything but sea salt, brine, and actinobacteria."

Åse frowned. "Actinobacteria?"

"Of course." Athena gave her a dubious look as though she should have known that. "The group of gram-positive bacteria that give caves their moldy, damp scent."

"Well, all I smell is dragon lust from other females who have been in his bed," Åse shot back.

More embarrassed by the moment, Athena went to step away, but he kept her close, not because he worried about her falling over but, shockingly enough, because he wanted to keep touching her. Comforting her if he could. He might not like Åse's intrusive ways, but he was grateful for her insight. It had never occurred to him to worry about other dragons' scents until now.

However, he could say with absolute disturbing certainty he would not want any other man's scent on Athena or her belongings. He knew, without question, it would infuriate his inner beast. That said, he also knew if he mated with her, theirs would be a monogamous partnership, which was startling indeed given his sexual appetites.

"I'm sorry, Athena," he said softly, well aware she lied about whose scent she'd caught last night because, at the very least, she had caught his. "I will see my bed furs replaced and my lair free of—"

"No." Athena shook her head. "That's not necessary." This time, when she stepped away, he reluctantly let her go. "This is *not* going to happen." She gestured between the two of them. "I can't be with a Viking dragon over a thousand years in my past and certainly not with one who craves battle and violence." She kept shaking her head. "It's too risky all the way around."

He was surprised and mildly amused when she stuttered on, saying things that made it clear she'd been giving the two of them some thought. Perhaps too much thought, considering they had only just met.

"Add to that the vast difference in our experiences with intimacy," she rambled on, gesturing loosely from Åse to him. "If she can't keep you satisfied, why would you ever think I could?" When she glanced warily from his groin back to his face, he knew she envisioned his untimely arousal earlier. "I've put off sex for a reason. When I do finally go there, it needs to mean something. I don't want to be one more in a long line of women." She frowned. "And honestly, when the time does come, I doubt I'll even like it."

"You will like it very much with Týr," Åse assured. "He is—"

"No," Athena snapped at her. She wagged her finger and narrowed her eyes. "Not another word from you about sleeping with Týr. Trust me, it's as bad if not worse than other females' scent in his bed."

A slow smile crept onto Åse's face. "So you *did* smell them."

"Actually, I mostly smelled you," Athena growled, surprising them both this time when her dragon eyes flared in warning. "So if you want what's best for Týr's cock as you put it, then you better stay the hell away from me *and* him."

While taken by her dragon eyes, he was also acutely aware his mood was shifting and his inner Helheim surfacing.

"I'd like to see you try keeping me away from him," Åse growled back, going for her dagger only for Athena to snag it first and hold it to Åse's throat so quickly she could have ended his friend before any of them had a chance to stop her.

When Ulrik and Keira headed their way, Týr put up a hand to stop them because he was curious to see how this played out.

"Do it, Athena," Åse taunted. A slow grin curled her mouth again, and her dragon eyes flared, challenging Athena as only Åse could. "End me now so I won't be a threat to you anymore. Show me you have what it takes to protect Týr. To be more than you've shown me thus far."

"Stop this, Týr," Rafe said into Týr's mind, clearly sensing trouble brewing from afar. *"Fire is heading your way, and it's feeding Athena's addiction. Making her unstable. You need to—"*

Rafe said more, but Týr couldn't hear him through the dark Helheim fluctuating within him. He was eager to see what Athena was capable of, even at the expense of his closest friend. Desperate to see her dragon fully surface and her blade cut.

"Enough, Athena," Keira said gently, resting a hand on Athena's shoulder. Her skin and eyes shined golden with her inner Valkyrie. "You need to fight what's happening inside you until you better understand it and do it *now.* Do you understand? Right *now.*"

"We've got incoming," Ulrik warned, pointing out the enemy dragons on the horizon. Sensing their intent, his cousin said words that soon made clear exactly where Týr's dragon stood when it came to the woman with a blade to Åse's throat.

"And they're coming for Athena."

Chapter Seven

ATHENA HEARD KEIRA'S warning to remove her blade from Åse's neck and fought to heed her, but her inner fury made reasonable thought next to impossible. She had never wanted to harm another human being as much as she did at that moment. Never wanted to run a blade she somehow knew how to use across another's throat for no other reason than she'd slept with Týr.

While she loathed the sensation, she craved violence and knew it had everything to do with her addiction to fire. She couldn't understand why until Keira bypassed diplomacy and knocked the blade out of Athena's grip.

Somehow, that snapped her out of it just in time to see what her inner beast had been up to beyond the obvious when four massive male dragons appeared on the horizon. While they certainly brought deadly fire with them, it seemed her dragon had an ulterior motive.

One so dangerous and convoluted she could hardly believe it.

"Oh, my *God*," she gasped, terrified but also awed when Týr leapt off the ship and embraced his dragon. Åse and Ulrik did, too, but all she could see was Týr as Keira, still glowing a shiny golden color, took up a defensive position in front of her. Regardless, she couldn't tear her eyes away from his massive black, muscular serpentine body and the blinding gold spikes on his tail.

She knew she should be terrified by what was about to unfold, but instead, a wicked thrill rushed through her, and heat burned her veins at the sight of him.

"This isn't going to be good," Keira muttered. "Týr's inner Helheim has too much control over him right now. More than that, he has too many to protect."

"What does that mean?" Athena asked, worried despite how attracted she was to him right now.

"It means he answers to no one but his inner Helheim." Keira scanned the skies for more enemy dragons. "And his Helheim will forfeit all to keep you safe."

"How do you know that?" She shook her head, confused. "I thought he was more level around me? I haven't even seen his other side."

"You would have a few minutes ago had your inner dragon given you half a chance." Keira held her blade at the ready as the enemy dragons closed in quickly. "But then she was playing all sorts of games, wasn't she?"

Though Athena knew she should feel guilty, the truth was that hadn't been her. Not really. Not any version of her she recognized anyway. And while half of her hated what her dragon had provoked, another side was mesmerized by seeing Týr like this.

Dark and lethal and out for blood.

"And completely out of control," Keira said through clenched teeth, following her thoughts. "Which means even Ulrik won't be able to rein him in."

Keira wasn't kidding because pure hell unleashed moments later when Týr roared and slammed into one of the larger enemy dragons, only for them to crash down into the sea. She leaned back against the railing on the ship's opposite side when it teetered dangerously from the wave borne of the impact, and icy water splashed over the side.

"Where is he?" Athena exclaimed in sudden, unexpected fear. She dodged around Keira and raced to the opposite side of the boat when it righted itself. For a split second, everything inside her went cold when the ocean's surface turned red with blood, but before she had a chance to panic, Týr shot out of the water and grabbed the neck of an enemy dragon who nearly made it to the ship.

Her jaw dropped as he snapped its neck and flung it down into the water. This time, she held on to the railing and braced her legs on the slippery, soaked deck as the ship teetered dangerously once again. Ulrik had just enough time to down the dragon he fought before Týr went after the fourth, which, unsurprisingly, Åse had already engaged.

She was doing well, too, considering this dragon was one of the largest, but she wasn't disposing of it fast enough for Týr's taste because he roared a long stream of fire at it, making Athena's knees weak with arousal. The enemy dragon had no time to recover before Týr roared more glorious fire, swooped around, and crashed into it so hard its back broke.

"Where is he going?" she exclaimed, still terribly aroused but also sickeningly fearful for Týr when he snagged the charred dragon out of the air and headed south.

"Don't go," she cried, hardly recognizing the agony in her own voice. Her vision hazed red again. "Come back!"

She had no real concept of what was happening to her other than she had to go after him. Follow him. Keep him safe. Protect him despite how clear it was, he could more than protect himself.

"Stop, *brennende en*," a deep, masculine voice murmured in her ear. A hard wall of muscle came against her back, and a warm hand wrapped around her arm where the baby dragon tattoo was. "Do not let your inner beast go after him. If you do, it will mean the death of you both. Far too many males will swarm you, and Týr *will* die defending you."

Her inner dragon flailed at the intimate contact from a male who wasn't Týr but simmered down as a strange yet comforting warmth spread through her. Half a breath later, the red faded from her vision, and she became embarrassingly aware a perfect stranger stood so close.

"My apologies," he rumbled in her ear, giving her no space to turn. "This is the only way to simmer your dragon down and get Týr back before it's too late."

"And is it, Rafe?" Ulrik grunted, appearing beside her moments later in human form. He scanned the horizon, troubled. "Will it work because I can't sense him?"

Rafe? As in their mystic cousin? When had *he* arrived? Not understanding what was happening, she tried to escape him, but he locked her firmly in place.

"Let me go!" she exclaimed, trying to see him over her shoulder, but from this angle, it was impossible.

"It will work," Rafe assured Ulrik. "*Is* working."

"What's working?" she fumed, getting more upset by the moment.

"That," Åse said, falling in on her other side. She gestured at the horizon with a strange mix of pride and disgust on her face. "Týr returns from taunting the enemy king out of petty jealousy over you."

She no sooner said it before Týr's dragon appeared on the horizon, looking mad as hell, minus the beast he had carried off. Madder than hell if such a thing were possible as he closed in on their ship.

"Are you up for this, Rafe?" Ulrik asked on a sigh. "His inner Helheim is still very much in charge, and we both know that makes him unstoppable."

"I have to be."

"Sword or axe because you know he'll come at you with an axe."

"Sword."

"Shield?" Åse asked.

"No."

"Should we step in at any point?" Ulrik asked.

"Only if there's no other recourse," Rafe replied. "He would never forgive himself if he killed me."

What were they *talking* about? What was the *matter* with these people? Týr wouldn't fight his own cousin over her...would he? And he certainly wouldn't kill him. Or so she hoped until seconds later, Týr was there, and it seemed they might just be right.

She spun the moment she was freed, only to see Týr crash down in human form with an axe in hand and a wild, furious look in his eyes when he locked onto the cousin who had been at her back seconds before. Meanwhile, Rafe, who was built much like his cousins, grabbed a sword midair that Ulrik tossed him and crashed blades with Týr.

Even though she was admittedly terrified by the pure violence that unfolded, she was also predictably mesmerized by it. She tried to fight the feeling, tried to remember how much she hated violence, but it was hard. So very hard. Týr was magnificent as he went after Rafe. Terribly arousing in the way his weapon almost became an extension of his arm.

He didn't whip his axe but used it with such skill against Rafe's sword a telling ache blossomed between her thighs. One mortifyingly enough, the man who had been against her back picked up on and used as ammunition, albeit a different type this time.

"Surely you must sense it is not me she desires, cousin," Rafe said, barely dodging Týr's methodical axe swings. "Surely you see she is safe now, and you yourself threaten such if you do not push past your Helheim. If you do not see reason."

"Reason?" Týr growled. "When you had her in your arms moments ago? In your arms as I defended her?"

"It wasn't willingly, not to mention he was goading you," she nearly said, but Keira touched her arm and shook her head, urging her to remain silent.

"*Why?*" she asked telepathically. "*Because Týr is misguided right now.*"

"*Týr is ruled by his inner Helheim right now,*" Keira clarified once again. "*Which means he is not seeing reason. Rafe can bring him back from that. Just let him do what he does best.*"

"*And that is?*"

"*Manipulate energies with Celtic magic is how Ulrik describes it,*" she replied as Týr and Rafe kept clashing blades. "*Typically, he draws on the power of his natural surroundings. In this instance, it's water which is more fluid than his main strength, the land and forest, but he will do it."* She shook her head. *"And you stepping in definitely won't help."*

Though she hated it and felt helpless, she heeded Keira because she was her best friend and she trusted her. Sure, she was a revered goddess now instead of a firefighter, but at the end of the day, Keira was dependable and trustworthy, and that had to be enough.

Fortunately, it turned out Keira was right because the more the men fought and Rafe kept talking, the less aggressive Týr became. And the less aggressive he became, the more the simmering beast that had reared its head inside Athena retreated to the back of her mind.

When that happened, the dark aura she'd caught pulsing around Týr subsided, and his fighting became more defensive than offensive before he frowned, blinked in confusion, then finally, at last, tossed aside his weapon.

"Loki's cock," he cursed, understanding what had happened. He took stock of his surroundings. Most specifically, Athena, it seemed, as his concerned gaze locked on her first before he sighed and clasped hands with Rafe in noticeable relief. "Thank you, cousin."

Rafe, who was just as handsome as the rest of them with dark chocolate brown hair and eyes that shimmered the color of the sea behind him, tossed down his blade, wiped sweat from his brow, and nodded. "You would do the same for me."

"I would," Týr agreed. "Always." She felt his wariness as he scanned the horizon. "How bad was it?"

"Bad," Ulrik said, clearly sensing unrest. "They were the dragon prince's beasts, and he's not happy."

"When is Magnus ever happy?" Åse spat, sneering at the horizon. "Traitor."

According to what Athena had learned regarding the ongoing strife in this era, it all began when King Knud's second-in-command ended the life of Zane's favorite mate several years ago. In his grief, Zane had one of Knud's most favored mates killed. After that, raids began between kingdoms, and allies became enemies, including Knud's sons, Magnus and Jørn.

It seemed Magnus turning on them was especially brutal, leading to bad blood between not just the Sigdirs and the dragon prince but Zane and Rafe. Their hatred for one another ran deep for reasons only they understood outside of the one reason Rafe, Týr, and Åse all took issue with him. His on-and-off recognition of Ulrik as king above kings.

Týr flinched when what he'd done under the influence of his inner Helheim seemed to come back to him. "I made it all the way to Magnus's shores before Rafe incited my dragon with Athena?"

By incite, he meant invoked jealousy.

"You did make it…just," Ulrik said, feeling out what they had been unable to see from the ship. His dragon eyes flared. "Rafe grabbed your attention right before you reached Magnus's kingdom, so you tossed the charcoaled body of his dragon warrior onto the shore for all to see."

"You mean for Magnus and his warriors to see so all would understand not to threaten my female again," Týr groused, obviously frustrated and discouraged by his actions. Showing yet another admirable aspect of his personality, he fell to a knee in front of Ulrik and lowered his head. "My deepest apologies, my King. I know this will not make the peace you strive to bring to our kingdoms any easier but far more difficult. To that end, I accept punishment in whatever form you see fit."

"Stand, friend." Ulrik frowned. "All you are guilty of is protecting your female against those who meant her harm, and that is not a crime." His voice became more of a growl. "May Magnus hear those words from afar and keep his beasts better tamed in the future."

Athena was about to pipe up and remind them she was *not* Týr's female, but Keira shook her head again and put a finger to her lips.

"But it's not true," she nearly argued telepathically, yet she lost her train of thought when she felt a strange sizzling sensation over her tattoo.

"We must go," Rafe cut in, clearly sensing the change in her tattoo, as well, because she stood somewhere else altogether seconds later.

Somewhere that showed her far more than she was ready to see.

.

Chapter Eight

TÝR FELT THE change in Athena's tattoo at the same time as Rafe and went to her the moment his cousin shifted them to the mystical standing stones behind his Stronghold. When he pushed up her sleeve to soothe her smoky skin, a jolt of awareness reddened his vision.

"What *was* that?" Athena whispered hoarsely, having felt it as well. "What just..."

She trailed off when her gaze fell to her tattoo.

"You recognize it then?" he said, running his finger over the swirling dragon that had replaced the baby one.

"I do," she murmured. "That's one of the dragons on your shield, isn't it? One that stands back-to-back with another dragon."

"It is," he confirmed, unsure what to make of it other than it backed up what he now knew without a doubt.

Athena *was* his.

His Helheim side had more than confirmed that, and while he hated letting his king down, he would do it again whether his inner

79

Helheim was at the forefront or not. Perhaps not so brutally, and hopefully without taunting his enemy, but even that he wasn't so sure of.

Not when it came to her.

"No," she said softly, shaking her head as she stared at the dragon in denial. "I can't be." Her wary gaze rose to his face. "*We* can't be."

"Yet you are whether your human half fully accepts it yet or not," Rafe said, joining them. "I have felt the tattoo and can confirm the dragon who created this is trying to remind you both of something dire. Something that will make all the difference." He looked at Athena. "Touch it, and you will see. *Feel*."

Athena frowned from Týr to the tattoo, but he felt her curious inner scientist win out before she rested her finger beside his on the dragon, and her pupils flared.

"It knows both of us," she whispered, following the sensation. "It…connects us somehow…is part of us…" Her gaze rose to his face. "Part of you."

"Yet still very much part of you." He nearly cupped her cheek in an intimate, almost loving gesture he'd never done to another but refrained. "*Us*."

She swallowed hard and pulled her hand away, but not before he felt her wariness and excitement. Part of her feared being destined for him, whereas another, most certainly her inner beast, longed for him in a way that affected her human half more by the moment.

"Welcome," came Ulrik's sister, Mea's soft voice before she appeared out of the mystical fog that frequented this place. Her long golden hair shimmered as she smiled warmly at Athena and introduced herself. "I see you are every bit as special as Keira."

"Does that mean she's Valkyrie, too?" Keira described to Rafe and Mea what had happened earlier between Athena and Åse. How Athena had not only stolen Åse's blade in a split second but pressed it to her throat before she even saw it coming. "Athena is every bit as fast with a blade as I am."

Mea and Rafe exchanged a look, and Mea replied on their behalf, as she tended to do on occasion because their magic was so aligned. "We cannot say with certainty until her magic fully ignites." She looked from a nearby standing stone to Athena. "Can you see the glow of the runic symbols?"

"No." Athena shook her head before she narrowed her eyes and drifted closer in awe. "But I *do* see *something*. Is that...water?"

Týr stuck close to her because he didn't trust her safety even in Rafe's Realm, a magical place others couldn't enter without Rafe and Mea's assistance.

When Athena touched one of the indentations in a runic symbol, he saw water trickling in it as well. She brought the tip of her moistened finger to her nose and sniffed. "Salt?"

When her dainty tongue flicked over the liquid, an all-too-familiar heaviness filled his cock, and he bit back a groan.

Fortunately, Athena seemed oblivious as she tasted it. "Salt water...sea salt." Her dragon eyes flared, and she clearly surprised herself when she pinpointed its origin through taste alone. "From somewhere in the Barents Sea..." Her eyes flared even brighter. "Water that's surrounding part of the seabed situated between land and deep sea...about twenty-five hundred meters down. A little under a mile."

"There *is* activity there," Rafe confirmed. "Volcanic in nature."

"Because it is a volcano," Athena murmured. "Only discovered in nineteen eighty-nine. They call it the Haakon Mosby mud

.66.24

.69

 .35

0

volcano. It's located halfway between the Norwegian mainland and what's known in my era as Bear Island."

"Is that where you think you hid Týr's shield?" Keira asked, frowning. "Underwater?"

"I don't know." Athena was about to go on but hesitated when the trickling water crystallized and turned to snow-caked ice beneath his fingertip.

"It's glacial ice," Týr exclaimed, certain of it.

When Athena touched it again, her inner dragon flared once more. "Yes, it is." She paused, sensing more. "It's from the Norwegian island of Jan Mayen, located in the Arctic between the coasts of Norway, Iceland, and Greenland."

"That location includes our other active volcano," Týr said. "Along with an extinct volcano."

"Right," Athena said slowly. "Beerenberg is the northernmost active volcano in the world, located in Nord-Jan. Sør-Jan, the southern part of the isle, hosts the extinct one."

"Do the runes show you any other extinct volcanoes?" Mea asked.

"No." Athena removed her hand. "So I can only assume I hid Týr's shield in one of those three locations." She shook her head. "Although, why would it show me three different spots for one shield? And if I hid it when I was in the twenty-first century, why would we find it in this era? Not to mention, how did I get it into one of these volcanoes when my dragon is only just surfacing now? Because it had to have been my dragon who did it."

"My guess is your inner beast has already surfaced, and you just don't remember it." Ulrik looked from Rafe to Mea. "Over the past few days, Rune has been giving her a magical brew that has ill-affected her from what I can tell."

"Or perhaps, from the sounds of it, prepared her," Mea said.

"I agree." Rafe eyed the incoming storm and gestured that they follow him. "Come inside and warm yourself so we might discuss this."

As expected, Athena was fascinated by Rafe's main cave.

"I thought the Yggdrasil in Týr's Lair was something, but these trees," she said upon entering, eyeing the branches far overhead, "these shouldn't be able to flourish like this here." She shook her head. "None of this should."

She took in the tree trunks growing up the walls and the broad canopy of green and autumn leaves covering the cave's ceiling.

"Even this is not quite right," Athena marveled, crouching at the edge of a crystal blue stream trickling through the cave. She touched one of several moss-covered rocks along its edges. "And this shouldn't like this area, yet it flourishes." A small smile curled her mouth. "Quinn needs to see this. She would love it...and understand it better."

"No," Rafe said softly, surprising them. "She should not come anywhere near this place."

Týr felt rather than saw how uneasy Quinn coming here made Rafe.

"Why?" Athena wondered, standing. "It seems so peaceful and beautiful."

"It can be for some," Mea said. "But not for others."

Týr wondered at the growing uneasiness in both Mea and Rafe but knew better than to ask about it. They would share more when they were ready.

"Well, Quinn's incredibly tuned into nature, so I'm sure—" Athena began, but Mea cut her off.

"We should discuss your upcoming journey," Mea said gently, gesturing at a long wooden table near the fire pit. "I sense you have not broken your fast yet this morn. Come sit and eat."

"Should we be worried about Quinn?" Athena said telepathically to Týr and Keira alone, which spoke to her emerging dragon's abilities. Or perhaps an already-emerged dragon still playing tricks.

"I wouldn't worry about her just yet," Keira said. *"This could just be a matter of Rafe not wanting to be destined for a modern-day woman."*

"I would think not." Týr wondered if they knew. *"Considering he's taken a vow of celibacy."*

Although shocked, they did well not to show it as everyone sat and enjoyed a freshly manifested array of food, from succulent meats to warm bread and sweet butter. They also did well to leave it at that, given they were in Rafe's magical realm. That meant he could very well cue into their conversation if he hadn't already.

"If Athena and Týr must go to the volcanoes she sensed in the standing stones," Ulrik eventually said, "I see but one way to go about it. Rafe will have to escort them because only he possesses the particular magic needed to protect them in such dangerous locations."

Týr sensed his king wasn't entirely pleased because they still didn't know if Rafe was the threat from within their own ranks, but they had little choice.

"Keira and I will remain here with Mea to protect the Stronghold, Fortress, and Týr's Dragon Lair against any retaliation attempts from the dragon prince, as I'm sure he sensed your presence on our ship as well, Rafe." Ulrik nodded once at Åse. "Because I know holding you back would be more of a chore than it's worth, you will go too and protect Týr, Rafe, and Athena with your life."

"Oh, I imagine Åse would much rather stay here and protect all of you," Athena argued, clearly not wanting her along.

"I will do as my King ordered and protect Týr and Rafe," Åse bit out, narrowing her eyes at Athena.

"*And* you will protect Athena," Ulrik reminded.

"*Ja*, my King."

"Åse?" Ulrik said.

"*Ja?*"

"Look me in the eyes when you say it so my dragon can see the truth of it."

Åse sighed and reluctantly met Ulrik's eyes. "Of course, I will protect Athena, my King." She shrugged a shoulder. "Which is really just protecting Týr because—"

"Good." Ulrik resumed eating. "Then it's settled."

"From what I saw on the ship," Keira added, backing up Athena, "I would say my friend might end up defending you in the end, Åse."

Åse offered nothing more than a snort, unconvinced.

"I would think you'd be impressed, Åse," Týr said aloud because he knew Athena would follow their telepathic conversation anyway. He gave his friend a pointed look. "I would also think by now you'd be of the mind that my mate is very likely Valkyrie as well, which would be an honor at the very least."

"Valkyrie or not, she has a dangerous addiction that could have gotten you killed back there." Åse manifested an ale and took several swigs bedamned the hour, speaking to just how concerned she'd been about him. "And an inner dragon that likes to play tricks."

"As much as I hate to say it again, she's right," Athena said a tad less meekly than she might have even a day ago. Rather, she squared her shoulders and met Åse's eyes. "So there. That's established. No need to keep repeating it as we move forward if for no other reason than I suspect I'll need to concentrate so I can

85

figure things out, including *why* my dragon's such a trickster. Do that, and I'll bet I'm one step closer to fixing it."

"We can only hope," Åse muttered. "Because if not, then—"

"So how do we do this exactly?" Athena said, redirecting the conversation Rafe's way. "Both areas are difficult, but as far as I know, the Haakon Mosby mud volcano is impossible to access. It's nothing but hot mud and methane gas."

"As far as your human half knows." Rafe's gaze flickered from her tattoo back to her face. "Your dragon clearly knows more, or you would not have been able to go there alone in the first place."

"Yet I *did* go there," Athena said softly, resting her hand over her tattoo. Týr was connecting with her so rapidly he sensed what she was about to say when she murmured, "Of course, there's more, but—" she shook her head— "you're right. Even my dragon should have had trouble going there."

When Keira looked at her quizzically, she went on.

"Where most underwater volcanoes are on the seabed of active continental margins—" Athena went to push now-gone glasses up her nose, only to remember they weren't there, so instead made a gesture, sliding one hand over the other— "you know, where an oceanic plate is forced under a continental plate." She shook her head. "That doesn't happen at Haakon Mosby because it sits on a passive continental margin."

"And that means what, exactly?" Keira asked.

"That passive continental margins have far fewer earthquakes, so things aren't as well defined," she said. "There's likely a system of fissures and magma chambers beneath the volcano that get filled and emptied. Deadly gas and suffocating mud go through them before there's a blowout. In the individual chambers, which may be as deep as a thousand meters below the seafloor, earthquakes *could* be activating things, but nobody knows for certain. The tide and changes in pressure could just as easily play a role in the volcano's activity." She shrugged as if she hadn't just painted a grim picture of their upcoming destination. "Either way, the area should be outright lethal for dragons, never mind humans."

Keira paled. "Please tell me you're not traveling to those chambers."

"I have a feeling we are," Athena said, not sounding all that frightened, but then, she clearly had a passion for this kind of thing. She looked at Rafe. "Though I can't imagine how we survive even with magic."

"In dragon form, for starters," Rafe replied. "From there, I should be able to handle things."

"*Should?*" Åse's eyebrows flew up. "That doesn't sound reassuring."

This time, Athena paled, but not because of facing certain death in muddy chambers far beneath the sea filled with poisonous gas but because of something that should be far less daunting. "I have to shift?"

"*Ja*, you have to shift," Ulrik said. "Even with Rafe's magic, our dragons couldn't withstand where you're going, which again begs the question, how was your dragon able to do it alone?"

"Assuming she was alone," Mea said. "Rune could have assisted her or someone else we're unaware of."

"You mean this unseen enemy you all have, don't you?" Athena said.

"It would be unwise to rule out anything." Mea gave her a reassuring look. "I do think if anyone else were capable of helping you get down there besides Rafe, it would most certainly be Rune."

"I agree," Týr said, wishing he and Athena sat beside each other rather than across from one another so he could touch her.

Comfort her. "Chances are even higher that it was Rune, given the tea she kept giving you."

"I agree as well," Ulrik said. "While I remain wary of Rune, I do think she is protecting you and your friends. That in mind, she seems the most likely candidate to have brought your dragon to all three locations."

"Which, again, points to me having shifted already." Athena shivered a little. "Although I can't imagine it."

Týr was about to reply when he caught something out of the corner of his eye. He blinked, trying to focus on it, only for a tiny blue dragon to appear, tiptoeing toward the stream.

"Athena," he whispered, certain it was her. Or maybe a ghost of her. So said the overwhelming emotion he felt at the sight of her. "She's here...you're here..." He couldn't help a small smile when the baby dragon stuck a tiny talon in the water and grinned at him expectantly before fading. "And I think I know what you have to do next."

Chapter Nine

"ARE YOU SURE the little dragon you just saw was me?" Athena asked Týr, shaking her head. "Because I'm certain I never shifted when I was younger."

"*Ja*, it was you." He was clearly touched by what he'd seen. "And I think she wanted to show me how to make shifting easier for you when the time came."

She tried to keep fear from her face because she didn't want to seem like a coward, but the idea of embracing her inner beast was terrifying. Mainly because she might put Týr in harm's way again.

"What if my dragon does something crazy?" She frowned at him. "What if she pulls your inner Helheim to the surface again?"

"I've been thinking about that." Keira glanced back and forth between them. "We assume your inner beast pulled that stunt with Åse on the ship so she could invoke Týr's inner Helheim and force him to embrace his dragon, therefore his fire, but what if her reasons weren't so nefarious?"

If only. "What do you mean? Because it felt really good—" she cleared her throat— "a little too good to see his dragon fire. Honestly, it felt like a fix for a fire addict."

"And it might have been in part," Keira conceded. "But what if it had more to do with drawing his dragon to the surface so he could do the same for yours? What if your fire addiction was solely to keep your dragon repressed until it was with its fated mate?" She didn't have to mention Athena's virginity to get her point across. "What if it affected aspects of your human half the same way?"

"That sort of thing has happened to other couples who came together across time," Ulrik said. "So it makes sense." He gestured at the stream. "And I think it's progressing if Týr just saw your baby dragon, whether you remember ever embracing your inner beast or not. It could be a manifestation your dragon wants him to see rather than an event that actually happened when you were young."

It seemed less and less odd to be having these conversations and more and more exciting somehow. Terrifying yet still exhilarating. Could Keira be right about her fire addiction having to do with reuniting with Týr? That would be something, *everything*, because it meant she could overcome it…maybe.

"Definitely," Týr said into her mind, a surprisingly reassuring and comforting presence the longer they knew one another. *"I will help you overcome anything that puts you in danger."*

Her cheeks warmed at how passionate he seemed about that. How much he meant it. *"You mean puts you in danger."*

"If you're out of danger, I'm out of danger," he reminded. He held out his hand and spoke aloud. "Come. Let me show you what I think your little dragon was trying to convey to me."

Should she? Dare she? What other choice did she have? And quite honestly, the building excitement inside her wouldn't have it any other way. So she slipped her hand into his, only to feel an electrical charge, or pleasant jolt, that made her feel incredibly alive.

"What *was* that?" she marveled, wondering if he'd felt it too.

"I think it probably has to do with what's coming." He knelt on one knee at the stream's edge and looked up at her. "Allow me to help you take off your boots?"

"Um…" She became acutely aware of the others watching them. "Couldn't you just chant them away?"

"I could." Her heart somersaulted when a slow smile crept onto his face. "But this moment feels like it deserves more than that."

This moment? One would think he proposed. She almost thought he was going to for a split second, especially when he wore the first smile she'd ever seen on his face. One that took him from out of her league to *way* out of her league.

"Okay," she managed, her voice sounding breathy even to her own ears as he encouraged her to rest her hand on his strong shoulder for support and took off one boot at a time. Breathing, let alone swallowing, became impossible when his warm fingers brushed her ankles each time. The sensitive arch of each foot. His touch was gentle and tender yet horribly arousing at the same time.

And he was merely touching her *feet*, no less.

"Are you alright?" he rumbled, sounding just as affected by the contact as he stood.

Not trusting her voice, she nodded.

"*Ja?*"

She stopped breathing altogether when he met her eyes and brushed the back of his fingers along her jaw. "Are you sure?"

She wasn't sure of anything anymore. Not how she could still be standing when she lost her breath at his touch or how her poor heart could withstand how loud it slammed inside her chest. Granted, she wasn't a doctor, but she was a scientist, so she knew things were too haywire inside her, so really, *technically*, she should probably be passing out about now.

Yet she wasn't. Hadn't. At least not yet.

Instead, she felt weak and strong all at once, and both sensations had everything to do with him as he encouraged her to step into the water.

Unsure how this would help her overcome her fear of shifting, she looked at him curiously. "Really?"

He gave her a reassuring look that leant not just strength but a strange sense of confidence and courage. "I'm almost certain."

"Okay." Rather than dwell on what might happen, and ever the scientist that just *had* to understand what made everything tick, she took the rhetorical leap and placed her foot in the cool water.

"I don't understand," she said once her foot was firmly on the soft pebbles, and pleasantly cool water swirled around her ankle, yet nothing happened.

Not at first, that is.

In fact, she was about to say more when images flashed in her mind. A snowy cold night overlooking Frenchman Bay in Maine. The golden glow of the Yggdrasil. The rocky shore beneath her very same foot. Icy water swirling around her ankle.

"Fly home, fiery dragon," Rune whispered into her mind. *"And hide it well."*

She blinked as the images faded, only to discover things had warped around her. Rather than looking up at Týr, she looked down at him. At least for a moment before, smoke swirled around him, and she looked up at him once more as he embraced his gorgeous black dragon. It took her a second longer to realize she'd embraced her dragon as well before their eyes locked for the first time in this form, and everything else faded away.

Then there was only them and a moment no scientific theory could explain.

It felt like she transgressed time and space in a singular moment without moving a muscle. As if she stared into eternity and back in the blink of an eye, and it was a thousand times more beautiful and impactful than anyone could ever have imagined.

"Hello, Athena," he rumbled into her mind. His deep dragon voice invoked such a delicious shiver she swore her scales rippled in pleasure. *"How do you feel?"*

"Terrified and powerful and...afraid to look anywhere but into your eyes." Then again, why would she want to when it felt like witnessing the Big Bang firsthand?

"Then don't until you're ready." He lowered his great head and shifted a tad closer, making her acutely aware of his masculinity, which should have been terrifying in this form but somehow wasn't. *"Take a moment to get comfortable and become familiar with your other half."* His cat-like pupils flared. *"Feel how stunning she is. How she is every bit as beautiful inside and out as her human half."*

Her scales warmed at the compliment, and she feared she'd crave the fire simmering inside them both, but she only sensed how he saw her and truly felt beautiful for the first time in her life.

When she was ready, because she knew she had to be, she dragged her eyes away and looked down at her shimmering silvery blue body. When she stared into the reflective surface of the stream, it was at a face she thought would terrify her, but instead, she saw a lovely creature staring back with eyes so incredibly sky blue they were startling.

"They're stunning," came a gentle voice beside her. "Just like you."

She wasn't sure how or why, but her dragon shifted her back to human form when she spied the older but lovely woman standing beside her.

"Oh, your dragon didn't need to do that," the woman said. She issued a small smile when Týr was suddenly there in human form on one side of her, and an older man who had to be his father based on their similar looks stood on the other, determined to keep her steady.

"I'm just a little weak these days," the woman went on, explaining the men's overprotectiveness. She squeezed Athena's hand affectionately in greeting. "Welcome, Athena." She looked from the older man beside her back to Athena. "We're Týr's parents, Dagr and Maya."

"So nice to meet you." Her heart went out to Maya, who wasn't doing well at all by the looks of it. Then it went out just as much to Týr and the worry and fear she felt radiating off of him when it came to his mother. "Please." Athena gestured at the table. "Come sit. Rest."

Maya went to take a step but faltered, so Dagr scooped her up and sat with her on his lap. He might have kept it from his face, but the terror Týr's father felt over his mate's illness was strong enough every dragon within a hundred-mile radius must feel it.

"You should not have come, Mother," Týr groused. "You should be resting."

He tried to lift a cup of water to his mother's mouth, but she batted it away before taking it from him. "I may be weak, but I'm not feeble, Son." Her words might be sharp, but the love she felt for Týr was palpable in the way she looked at him. "You know better than to think I wouldn't come meet your fated mate and see you off on such a dangerous venture?" Although there was steely strength in her gaze as it went from Athena to Týr, there was also genuine worry. "Because it *will* be exceptionally dangerous."

Although there was nothing stranger than having the mom of a man she'd met days before call her his fated mate, she knew now wasn't the time to deny it. If anything, now was the time to pay attention to what Maya and Dagr said because they had things to share. She was certain of it.

The others remained quiet, but she sensed their sadness and worry over Maya's condition. For the first time since arriving in tenth-century Norway, she felt how deeply connected these Vikings actually were, thanks to finally embracing her dragon in a way that went beyond Rune's influence. Because wherever Athena had hidden the shield, it had been undoubtedly thanks to Rune, at least in part. Why, though? What did Rune know that they didn't?

Better still, what did Athena's dragon know?

"It's about the shield, isn't it?" she said softly. "It always meant more than the sword that came with it."

"Yes," Maya confessed. She looked at Týr with a sigh as he sat across from them beside Athena. "The sword was merely a gift from me and your father—" the corner of her lip curled up as she took in the axe strapped to his back— "even though you've always secretly preferred battling with an axe."

"It is a good sword," he conceded, meeting her small smile. "But yes, I battle better with my axe."

Did he *ever*. Athena tried not to envision how mesmerizing he had looked fighting Rafe on the ship. She squeezed her thighs together and did her best to set aside how arousing the mere memory made her because now was most certainly not the time for it.

"And the shield?" Athena persisted a bit hoarsely, hoping no one caught her arousal because she felt an affinity to them all growing more by the moment. A primal synchronization if she were to put it in scientific terms. Like cells merging and becoming one yet still somehow separate entities.

"The shield was given to us by Loki to give to Týr," Dagr replied when Maya sipped her water, clearly dehydrated. "That much is true." He looked at his son. "But there was more to his message. An additional message if you found yourself seeking the shield someday. A shield stolen by another, a mate, who purposely hid it."

"And that is?" Týr prompted when his father hesitated, clearly undaunted by the implication Athena might be his mate.

"That when you find it, you must be willing to sacrifice all for her," Maya said softly, pained by her admission based on the saddened look in her dragon eyes when they locked on Týr. "You must be willing to sacrifice not just your life for her but the world as you know it."

"Absolutely *not*." Athena shook her head and frowned from Týr to his parents. "When I arrived at the Maine chalet, I felt there was something there that would make the world a better place. Is that what this is about?" Her brow furrowed. "Even though I suppose it could mean the opposite." She clenched her fist on the table and ground her jaw, giving in to both her inner dragon and human's strong denial. "Whatever it means, and I can't stress this enough, absolutely *not*. I won't allow Týr to die for me."

Trying to squelch panic that had everything to do with the thought of his death, she looked from Týr to his parents and went on. "Why would a god who's supposed to be your friend require that?" Feeding off his repressed emotions, she looked directly at Ulrik. "Even though Loki's not your friend anymore, right? Since its been proven the peace he promised you after the Great War was a lie, given the state of your kingdoms these days?"

"You speak *blasphemy*," Åse ground out, glaring at Athena before, surprisingly enough, she pounded a clenched fist on the table and nodded once that she too would be blasphemous when her angry gaze went to Týr's parents. "Yet I stand by Athena in this. Why would Loki demand this of a loyal warrior who has only ever stood by his homeland? By his *true* king and gods?"

"We cannot say." Maya gave Åse a stern but compassionate look. "Either way, is it not our duty to heed the gods? Heed Loki especially?"

"I heed no—"

"*Enough.*" Týr might be frowning at Åse, but Athena felt his pride knowing she continued to stand by his side. Regardless, he'd only let her go so far, so he narrowed his eyes at who Athena now understood, thanks to her inner dragon, was truly his best friend. "There is no reality on all of Midgard or the other eight worlds where I would allow you to speak against the gods on my behalf, Åse. Know that and know it well, woman, or you will *not* continue on this journey with me and my mate."

Yet again, Athena nearly said she wasn't his mate, but once more, this wasn't the time. Because if she'd figured out nothing else after Maya and Dagr's revelation about the shield, it was that she wanted anyone who would die for Týr to remain with them going forward, and Åse was right there at the top. Only one rung down from Athena if the emotions rocketing through her inner dragon were anything to go off.

"Besides," Týr went on, "we all know Loki is known for tricks and riddles, so his warning is open to interpretation." He sighed. "There is much to consider here." Clearly conflicted by Loki's prophecy and loyalty to his king, Týr's gaze went to Ulrik. "There's much I must discuss with my king."

"Indeed," Dagr said, his gaze wary when he looked Ulrik's way because he and he alone was the only one with the power to stop this if they were lucky. Yet Athena sensed it was too late for that.

Even so, Ulrik nodded and gestured for Týr to join him in another cave that ran alongside the one in which they sat. Invited him to have a discussion Athena and Åse both knew as they, for the first time, exchanged a look that wasn't against each other, that the matter was entirely out of their hands, and the outcome would likely be horrific.

Chapter Ten

TÝR HAD NO idea what to say to his king as they went into Ulrik's cave in Rafe's Realm, where he knew no one could hear them, be it telepathically or otherwise. All he knew was they needed to talk, and he had to try his best not to undo the peace Ulrik had long worked toward more than he already had.

"Yet that will not be your main concern in the end," Ulrik led with, naturally following his thoughts as they stood before another fire. "Not when it comes to keeping your mate safe." He stared into the flames and sighed. "Trust me, I know this well. If your dragon is convinced Athena is his, your human half will be helpless to do anything but keep her safe."

Týr frowned. "Surely not if it means destroying all you have worked toward because we both know Loki's warning about sacrificing myself for Athena and the world as I know it could easily mean outright war."

"Or it could mean certain peace because that's clearly not the world we know at the moment, either," Ulrik pointed out. "Either way, nothing else will matter when it comes to protecting your mate, be it war or peace or even the end of dragonkind." He met Týr square in the eyes. "To give you some perspective, as much as I love and respect you, I would cut you down at this very moment if you threatened Keira's life in any way." He shook his head. "There would be no hesitation or thought to our past and deep bond. Only ever a need to keep her safe because that's what it is to become fated mates with another dragon."

"Yet Athena and I are not fated but merely mates," Týr replied despite already knowing Ulrik was right. Despite knowing deep down nothing, not even his king and people, dragonkind, or even mankind, would stand in his way of protecting Athena.

He had begun sensing it before he saw her shift for the first time, but now...now everything had changed. How could it not when he'd seen her stunning silvery blue dragon? Looked into her near-blinding sapphire eyes for the first time?

His dragon had been so humbled and aroused it was a wonder it hadn't tried to mount her then and there. A wonder still since it had felt such tenderness and respect, it refrained from pouncing on a virginal female because his lust had been remarkable. Yet his need to keep her safe, even from what his beast wanted to do to her, to ease the ache it felt at seeing her, was far stronger.

"If you saw Athena's baby dragon, chances are good you are fated mates." Ulrik eyed Týr wisely. "But I suspect you already know that and battle with your inner beast even now. It will be a losing battle, too, my friend. That said, there is only one way to handle this." His cousin gestured at the ground. "Kneel before your king."

Although Týr frowned, not liking where this was going, he was not Zane but loyal to his one true king, so he fell to a knee and lowered his head.

"Swear to me now that you will protect Athena at all costs, no matter what it takes." Ulrik rested his hand on Týr's shoulder and said words that both broke his heart yet freed him at the same time. "Swear to me you will let nothing stand in the way of that. Not me, our people, mankind, or even dragonkind. That you will remain true to why Loki entrusted you with your shield."

"I will *not* see everything you have worked toward undone," he tried to push past his lips, but the words caught in his throat. "I *refuse* to let you down," he tried to say, but again, the words would not come. Not when all he could see was the freedom of being able to protect Athena, whatever it may take.

Even if it meant burning down the world around him.

"Swear to me, cousin," Ulrik ground out, the power in his voice unmistakable before his tone softened. "Promise me, friend. For if I cannot trust you to do my bidding, who *can* I trust?"

"No one," he managed, knowing it to be true. They had been unwaveringly close since childhood, and that would not change now. *Could* not if it were the last thing he did.

"Good," Ulrik said, following Týr's words, both spoken and unspoken. "Then raise your head and swear your fealty, human to human and dragon to dragon."

"Once I do that," he warned, "there is no turning back."

"Nor should there be." Ulrik hesitated a moment before continuing. "Nor would you be the man, dragon, or warrior I know you to be if you didn't protect what is dearest to you, and that can only be your mate even above me. In fact, I would think less of you if you did not do as I would in your position. If you did not stand by love."

Týr startled at the use of that word. More so, the strange sensation that rolled through him when he heard it in relation to Athena. He started to say so, too, that he hardly understood love outside of how he felt about kin but, again, couldn't push the words past his lips.

It did, however, somehow make it easier to say what Ulrik needed to hear.

"I swear," he vowed, feeling a change in his inner beast almost immediately. "I will stand by Athena no matter what it entails." When his vision hazed red with his inner dragon, he raised his eyes to Ulrik and meant every word with an intensity he didn't anticipate. "I will protect her with my life and well beyond into Helheim, forfeiting the great halls of Valhalla if it means keeping her safe."

"Good." Ulrik nodded once, accepting his loyalty to another. "May you keep your mate with you always." He held out his hand. "Then, upon your return, help me reunite our kingdoms once and for all."

"Do not doubt it for a moment, my King." Týr lowered his head once more, then clasped his cousin's hand and stood, welcoming his embrace, then an ale when he handed it to him.

"You leave very soon," Ulrik said, "so let us share this last drink together first, *ja?*"

"*Ja.*" He held up his horn. "Skald, my King!"

"To a safe journey, my friend." Ulrik managed a smile and raised his horn in return. "Skald!"

And so, they drank and talked for several too-short minutes, but it was enough to address another concern.

"Are you sure we should travel with Rafe?" Týr asked. "Do you trust him, given we still don't know who the betrayer is amongst our own?"

"You ask that when you are so convinced it is Zane?"

"I ask that because it needs to be asked," he said. "I do not think Rafe would ever betray you, *us*, but it would comfort me to hear you say the same."

"I do not think he would, either," Ulrik said without hesitation. "Enough so, I trust sending him with you and Athena. Trust him to protect you with his magic and his life."

That was an awful lot of trust, considering where they were going. Yet it was trust Týr needed, so he nodded, and they made quick work of their conversation and drink as journeying by day was safer than by night, and daylight hours were shorter this time of year.

The moment they reentered the main cave, he felt an overwhelming relief at laying eyes on Athena again. Knowing she was safe despite being among allies in a place so thoroughly protected by Rafe's magic.

He could tell she felt the same by how she looked at him despite her nervousness and excitement. That would be what kept her going above all, he realized. The curiosity of her profession because, first and foremost, she was a scientist at heart, so the concept of traveling where no scientist could and discovering things unknown to man, made her come alive almost as much as his presence.

He was neither arrogant nor wrong with that assessment, and it pleased both sides of him greatly. Whether she knew what to do with it yet, Athena desired him as much as he did her. More than that, she looked forward to what came next between them. That, naturally, made him pray it would be something far better than a fiery death at the hands of unpredictable gaseous chambers beneath a deep-sea mud volcano.

Dragons could deal with much, but volcanoes, be they above or below ground, could be tricky and dangerous for their unpredictability. Dragon fire was one thing. It was fierce but brief, where volcanic fire and lava were ceaseless and patient, with the ability to trap a dragon like a spider trapped its prey in a web. Patient as it waited out an inevitable death because even dragons could only take flames for so long.

"We should go soon," Rafe said, echoing Týr and Ulrik's sentiments. "I can get all four of us off the coast in dragon form, but then it will be—"

"No," Athena said softly, resting her hand over her tattoo as if it guided her. "That's not the way to go." She blinked as if seeing something in her mind's eye. Something that rose up within Týr's mind as well, and she knew it when she looked his way. "Where is that? Because that's our way in...then down..."

"Down?" Keira said, clearly uncomfortable. "What do you mean?"

"I can't believe this," Athena murmured, clearly caught between dragonly knowledge and a scientific discovery. "It was *right* there all along. Right there on the shores explorers and scientists sailed from to get to the mud volcano." She nodded as though talking to herself. "Hidden caves on the southwest Norwegian coastline that lead down to..."

When she trailed off, Týr knew she understood, and Rafe confirmed it.

"No." Rafe shook his head. "That is on Magnus's land, and given today's events, the dragon prince is angrier than ever."

"Yet the prince does not possess your magic when it comes to land or caves, even in his own territory," Týr's mother reminded. "His magic is wild and without grounding these days." She nodded once in reassurance. "You can get by him, nephew, and you know it."

"She's right," Dagr said. "Magnus is consumed with rage right now and likely not thinking clearly." He looked from Týr to Rafe. "Use that to your advantage."

Athena frowned. "What does that mean exactly?"

"It means Ulrik and I are going to distract him in an attempt to make peace," Keira said firmly despite her inner turmoil at her mate being put in harm's way. "When we do, you four are gonna make a run for it straight down into deep-sea hell, for lack of a better way to put it."

"No." Athena shook her head and rounded her eyes on Keira. "That's way too dangerous, and you're pregnant!"

"But she's also Valkyrie," Dagr said, clearly not pleased but saying what needed to be said. "And it's time our real enemies know that." He lowered his head to Keira. "*Respect* that."

"I agree," Maya said. Even though she nodded to his father that she was okay to stand, he remained by her side along with Týr as she made her way to Rafe and cupped his cheeks. Looked at him with pride and faith. "If anyone can get my boy and his mate where they need to go, it's you." She narrowed her eyes. "*You*, Rafe." She shook her head. "So enough worrying about enemies and do what you *truly* do best above all. Become one with the land. You might be traveling beneath the ocean, but you'll be underground, and that is *Midgard*." Her dragon eyes flared. "That is *you*."

If anyone could give Rafe the confidence he needed, it was one of their matriarchs, which became clear in the subliminal shift he felt around his cousin when he looked at Keira, understanding she would always stand by Ulrik. "Are you sure about this, my Queen?" He looked at Ulrik. "My King?"

Ulrik nodded without hesitation, proving to Týr he truly did believe Rafe wasn't their hidden enemy. "We are." Where most would do anything to keep their mate away from danger, they need only know Keira mere minutes to understand she'd never allow it pregnant or not. Yet Ulrik gave her a say always and likely secretly hoped she'd say no. "*Ja, mektig kriger?*"

"*Ja*," Keira confirmed. She embraced Athena when she looked uncertain, then held her at arm's length, her dragon eyes flaring. "I'll be just fine, but will you? Are you ready for this? Because fire might be involved even though Ulrik and I aim for diplomacy."

Athena's dragon eyes flared in response. "I am."

She nodded and squared her shoulders a little as if testing out the strength he felt filling her. An inner dragon she now realized could surface without laying fiery waste to everything. More so, she sensed it wasn't craving fire quite as much as it had before. At least not the kind of fire she could find twenty-five hundred meters below the sea surface.

"I can do this," Athena said, sounding certain as she went on.

"Yeah?" Keira pressed, not willing to chance it. "Even if it means embracing your dragon? Rafe will get you there in human form, but you'll have to shift to survive the deeper you go." Keira squeezed her shoulders. "Then, after that, you'll have to fly as your journey continues. I can't imagine any way around it ."

"I know." Athena managed a small smile. "Not sure if you've caught it along the way, but fire's always been the bigger issue."

"Right." Keira met her smile. "Okay then." She pulled Athena in for another tight embrace. "You got this."

"I do." Athena embraced her just as tightly. "As long you stay safe, too, I do."

"I will." Keira pulled back and looked from Rafe to Åse before her gaze landed on Týr. "Take care of her."

"With my life," he swore, never meaning anything more before he embraced his parents goodbye and shook his king's hand one last time, saying with a look what he could not put to voice.

Stay safe and protect their kin and people with everything in him if Týr did not come home.

"You will, though," Athena whispered into his mind. "*I won't have it any other way.*"

While some might say it was her inner Valkyrie simmering beneath the surface, he sensed it was far better than that. It was her dragon. Better still, her human. Which said much because he knew, one way or another, her logical, scientific human mind was the biggest hurdle.

"So what's next?" Athena asked. "What should I expect when—"

Before she could finish her sentence, Rafe transported them into enemy territory. Týr brought her against his front and wrapped a gentle hand over her mouth before she uttered another word. As far as he could tell, they were inside the caves Athena had just referred to.

"*As I'm sure you already figured out, Rafe isn't known for finesse but expediency once he sets his mind to something,*" he whispered into her mind telepathically. "*Now, stay silent until he gets us beyond the range of enemy ears.*"

He knew what he did next wouldn't please her, but there was no help for it. She wasn't familiar enough with her surroundings to move fast.

"*Any more than you are,*" she exclaimed, dodging him in the darkness before he had a chance to scoop her up and carry her. "*And I am familiar with my surroundings,*" she gasped, clearly using her dragon eyesight as she peered around the dark, dank cave. "*I know this place.*"

"How well?" Rafe asked. "*While I can use my magic sooner rather than later, it would be more favorable if you knew the way and led us until we get out of enemy territory lest they detect my powers.*"

While not the leadership he had hoped for from his cousin, he sensed rather than saw the wisdom in it soon enough because even underground magic could be detected, especially at so shallow a depth.

"I do know the way," Athena confirmed, marveling at her surroundings. *"Because I've been here before."*

When Rafe and Åse looked at Týr, he knew what they were wondering without sensing it in their mind. Would he let his mate lead the way? Was he ready for that?

"Like I assured Keira, I've got this," Athena said with admirable determination, clearly catching their concern. *"In fact, I get the feeling I've been ready my whole life."*

Týr went to ask her if she was sure, but it was too late.

Athena was on her way into what could very well be certain death, and there was no stopping her.

Chapter Eleven

MAKING HER WAY down into the damp caves that would lead them to the mud volcano felt like waking from a dream. Or was it remembering a dream? As strange as it was, Athena knew it was a little bit of both, thanks to Rune's tea.

She could hardly believe she was grateful for Rune's meddling. At least at the moment, as she made her way effortlessly along, marveling at how the tunnel looked with her dragon sight. How the crystalized volcanic rock shimmered like quartz, casting prisms here and there.

Though she led the way, Týr often assisted her in steep areas. While she appreciated it, every time he took her hand, she felt that same intense jolt of awareness she'd felt back in Rafe's cave. A pleasurable current that made her acutely aware of him.

In fact, she was so aware of him that while she should be completely absorbed by everything around her and where she was going, her thoughts were more focused on him at her back. His scent. The way his footsteps fell in such a way she knew he was poised to catch her if she tripped. How he gripped his axe every so often as though making sure it was still there so he could cut down anyone who might try to harm her.

Shockingly enough, because what she headed toward was every volcanologist's dream, she found him far more interesting than the marvels ahead. More compelling than anything ever, if she were to be honest, and it was a strange revelation.

"I couldn't agree more," he said telepathically, so in tune with her now she knew he followed most of her thoughts. That would have mortified her before, but not now. Instead, it made whatever this was developing between them easier. Better.

Or so she thought until his next rather straightforward question. But then Týr did have a way of cutting to the quick.

"Why have you not lain with a man yet, Athena?" he wondered. *"Setting aside it might have been your inner dragon influencing you, I wonder why your human waited because I don't think it was entirely what you claim. I don't think it was simply because you wanted it to be meaningful."*

"Is this really the best time to talk about this?" she wondered as they descended beneath the sea. Based on her popping ears, the pressure was changing, and it wouldn't be long before they would have to shift.

"I cannot see why it matters when or where we talk of your virginity," he replied. *"I thought perhaps while we have this time…"*

When he trailed off, she understood, and it made her chest tighten in sudden fear and sadness. Because of what he'd learned from his parents about dying to protect her, he feared their time together would be brief. In truth, she feared it every bit as much, and it hurt. Really, truly hurt. So she talked and shared things she never thought she would with a man, let alone a male dragon.

She spoke of the misfit she'd been in foster care growing up and how she'd been bullied in her teenage years. How boys hadn't looked at her like they did other girls, and that had not changed much since.

"*Eventually, my studies and science just became more important, I guess,*" she said in conclusion because her love life from start to finish had been pretty unexceptional. "*I found acceptance and respect in my field, and that's all that mattered. Sure, I like to date, but it never goes much beyond those first few dinners before they ghost me.*"

"*What is this they do to you?*" Týr grunted, clearly displeased. She could sense him clutching his blade again as if ready to cut down whoever had hurt her.

"*Ghost me,*" she said. "*No worries, it doesn't mean they physically hurt me. Just that they didn't call back and never responded to my texts.*" She shrugged as she made her way between two boulders. "*They simply vanished from my life, telling me everything I needed to know.*"

"We should shift now," Rafe said as he sidled past Athena. His voice sounded oddly muted when in a tunnel beneath the sea. "And I will lead now."

While tempted to argue, she knew it was for the best because she didn't remember much beyond this point, so there was no way to know what they faced ahead.

"Are you ready?" Týr rumbled, resting his hand on her shoulder.

He might be well-meaning and concerned, but her breath still caught at how closely he stood behind her. How heat fanned beneath her skin at his touch, however platonic the gesture.

"This will be different than shifting in Rafe's Realm," Týr went on, the gruffness of his voice telling her he wasn't unaffected by their contact either. "Far different."

111

"I'll be okay," she said, certain in a way she shouldn't be if she hadn't done this before. She glanced over her shoulder into his dragon eyes and nearly lost her footing but managed to lock her knees first. "I'm sure of it."

He searched her eyes as if seeking out any waver in her assurance before shocking her when he cupped her cheek and brushed his lips across hers. It was quick, too quick by far, but it impacted her so strongly her locked knees just about gave out.

"I will never ghost you, Athena," he promised softly, holding her gaze. "And that, as you put it, should also tell you everything you need to know." He nodded once, giving her strength she didn't realize she needed outside of the obvious. "Now shift and follow Rafe. I will be right behind you always. With you always."

She nodded but couldn't quite get a reply out.

"Go," he urged gently, clearly pleased his kiss had affected her so strongly. He gestured ahead. "Show me what one of these volcanoes you love so much looks like."

Finally snapping out of whatever spell he'd cast her under, she managed to nod and focused on the tunnel ahead. She thought, at first, she would have no idea what to do next because this was different than stepping into a stream and having flashbacks, but somehow it wasn't as Rafe shifted and his dragon headed downward, clearly in its element surrounded by rock. Such beautiful rock she was suddenly eager to experience in a whole new way, so she leapt after him only to feel her body change. Shift. Become better and stronger.

Traveling in her human form in this tunnel was one thing. In dragon form, another altogether. Where the rock had been beautiful before, now it was beyond magnificent. Utterly glorious as its colors cascaded around her. Racing through the tunnel now felt like pure joy. Like coming home in some strange way.

"Because you are," Týr said into her mind, his dragon voice even more arousing than it had been before. *"Caves and mountains are natural habitats for dragons. Rock and the shelter it provides has always been most kindred to our kind."*

"I see that. Feel that." She zipped along, loving how her serpentine body moved. *"It's truly amazing."*

And it should be studied more, in her opinion. Dragons from her era didn't keep lairs or dwell in caves, to the best of her knowledge. Maybe some, but she didn't know them.

"We're getting close to the network of chambers beneath the volcano," she said telepathically to everyone. *"And it's definitely not a place for our human halves."*

"No," Rafe agreed, clearly sensing the same. *"Once we infiltrate it, time will be limited, even for our dragons, so we will have to find a place to rest for the night before attempting it."*

"Why?" She bit back disappointment. *"If we're so close, why not do it now?"*

"Because the sun lowers soon," Týr said. *"And we cannot risk being weakened by the volcano, then flying at night. It's far too dangerous."*

"So where do we stay..." she began, only for that same sense of *déjà vu* to overcome her. The sensation told her she'd been here before. *"Rafe, there's a tunnel to your right up ahead. Take that instead of going straight."*

"Are you sure?"

"Positive," she replied. *"Our humans can find shelter there for the night."*

"So close to the volcano?" he returned dubiously.

"Yes, as long as you can help us handle the pressure of the water above us," she said. *"Trust me."*

Fortunately, he heeded her advice, and within minutes, the tunnel she'd recommended led them to a large, spacious cave with several smaller caves beside it. Its rock walls were relatively smooth and rich with magnesium, iron, and calcium, implying these caves had likely experienced high-temperature melts at one time. Been the brunt of impossibly hot, fast-flowing magma.

"How is this possible?" Åse wondered as Rafe assured them it was safe to shift back to their human forms. She gazed around, trying to understand. "Why is the air so much better here?" She inhaled deeply. "I cannot even smell the noxious gasses that permeated the tunnels."

"It's most definitely a natural wonder," Athena marveled, pointing up at several openings overhead that ran in the opposite direction and whistled with what sounded like wind. "I would guess those lead to much smaller tunnels that reach different areas of the shoreline, allowing fresh air to fill these caves. Their position aiming away from the volcano keeps this location methane-free." She shook her head. "This is an unexplored location no scientist could ever travel to unless they were with a dragon like Rafe."

"And not such a bad place to rest," Týr said, taking in their rather glorious surroundings. The ceiling was cathedral-like, and the elements in the rocks down here were more stunning still by dragon sight. "Then we will press on first thing in the morn."

"Ja." Rafe manifested a small fire for light rather than out of necessity because heat wasn't needed. Caught between the frigid water above and the molten heat close by, they were in a bit of a Goldilocks zone. "Let us eat and rest soon."

With that, he manifested a table with food and ale.

"Do you not want water?" Týr asked her as they sat, and Athena eyed one of the mugs of ale. "Because you don't drink alcohol anymore, ja?"

"I don't," she said softly, sniffing the Viking ale curiously. "But only because I was afraid of what my dragon might do if I did."

"A valid concern," Åse muttered around a piece of bread before she swallowed and narrowed her eyes at Athena and the ale she contemplated. "Should it be assumed your inner dragon caused others harm with fire when last you drank?"

"It doesn't matter what it did," Athena said absently. "What matters is things seem to be changing since I embraced my inner beast at Rafe's. I haven't craved fire or violence in the least."

Not really. Not enough to worry about.

"Is it so wise to test that with ale now?" Rafe wondered, equally concerned. "We are very close to an immense amount of trouble if your dragon misbehaves, not to mention we still don't know who brought you here initially. While all signs point to Rune, I have seen my cousin Zane do unthinkable things, so he must not be ruled out. He may know you are here at this very moment, which means he or one of his deviants might be watching and waiting."

Athena understood all that. She truly did. But it didn't override what had occurred to her the moment she'd remembered this cave existed. Did not sway her from wanting to take advantage of what could very well be their last night alive.

Týr's last night alive if Loki's dire warning was anything to go off.

With that in mind, she had come to a swift decision and wondered if Týr had picked up on it yet. More than that, she wondered if he would agree to it.

Chapter Twelve

THE MOMENT TÝR figured out Athena intended to lie with him that night, he had trouble focusing on much of anything. Instead, he did his damndest to keep his cock from swelling with anticipation. Even when Athena claimed she wanted to try some ale in such a precarious location.

"Are you hoping it will give you courage?" he said into her mind. *"Because I sense what you're determined to do this eve, Athena."*

"Maybe a little bit," she confessed. Her cheeks turned rosy in embarrassment, but at least she looked at him rather than avoiding eye contact. *"But also, because it's something I simply want to try before it might all be over."*

He sensed the truth in her inner words and could not blame her on either count. So he recommended she fill her belly first so the ale wouldn't affect her as strongly.

"So, is anything coming back to you about what we might expect in the volcanic chambers tomorrow?" Rafe wondered as they ate. "Perhaps if there's a way out other than the way we came in?" He flinched. "And other than the way the methane goes out."

"I'm afraid not," Athena replied. "Hopefully, the longer I'm down here, the better the chances I'll recall something."

Týr did his best to focus on the ongoing conversation that mostly revolved around Athena providing a scientist's description of their surroundings, from the copper, zinc, cobalt, gold, and silver in the rock to the ocean's density above them. Even though her wealth of knowledge was admittedly fascinating, it did little to keep his focus on anything but the way she licked her lips every so often and what those lips might be capable of when they were doing far more enjoyable things.

The way she'd responded to a mere brush of his lips earlier made him eager to see how she would react to far more. Interestingly, however, he wasn't just experiencing an overwhelming need to taste the juices between her thighs and sink into her welcoming body, but he longed to taste her sweet lips again. To slip his tongue into the warm recesses of her mouth. All thoughts he knew she caught based on her ceaseless blush and uneven breathing.

"Come, Athena," he eventually said once they finished eating. He had never been so impatient for anything. "Let us find a quiet area for you to enjoy your ale before we rest."

Åse and Rafe were no fools and understood what was happening, which was not such a bad thing for several reasons. First, lying with Athena could only ever keep him level. Second, it was well-known dragon mates tended to find extra strength, especially of the magical variety, once they connected mentally *and* physically with their other halves.

"No, not that way," Athena said, surprising them both when she veered off in another direction. He had to bend over to get down the narrow tunnel they traversed, but the small cave she led him to was worth it for its privacy alone.

"This is *amazing*," she murmured, awed as she stared up at the glittering cave ceiling. An eerie-sounding wind whistled from somewhere unseen and lent a pleasing breeze where he would have never thought one possible.

Eager to make the place more welcoming than Athena already found it, he manifested several thick furs and pillows alongside a small fire. He felt how nervous she was growing, so he sat on the furs with his back to the wall, manifested two cups of ale, and patted the spot beside him.

"Come sit, Athena," he said gently, somewhat amazed he could manage anything but ravishing her at the moment. Doubly amazed, he was able to keep his erection under control, without a doubt, thanks to his inner beast not wanting to frighten her. "And remember, we don't need to do this." He shook his head, damning his words because they might keep her out of reach, but he meant them. He would only have her if she wanted him in return. "You can change your mind at any time."

"I won't." Her voice was a little shaky as she sat beside him and took her cup. "I just need to..." She shook her head, swallowed hard, and took a small, tentative sip of ale. "Brace myself, I guess."

"You need not this first time." He assumed she thought he would begin by mounting her a certain way. "I will not take you roughly until you are ready for it."

She choked a little on her ale but managed to get it down before she issued a wobbly smile. "Um, that's not quite what I meant by bracing myself."

Glad to see her smile, he perked his brows, prompting her to explain.

"I just meant I was preparing myself mentally for such a big moment." She took another small sip and eyed him with concern. "And just a general FYI, I'm fairly certain I'll never want to do it roughly." She cleared her throat before rallying on. "Have you ever been with a virgin before, Týr? Because it's...what I mean to say is it's pretty daunting on my end...especially with someone like you."

He didn't need to ask what she meant by that because he knew she was generally attracted to men like John. Frail humans who wouldn't know the first thing about how to please her properly. No idea how to worship her body the way it should be worshiped.

"No, I have never lain with a virgin." He drank from his ale and shrugged. "If I were to be honest, until I met you, I probably would not have known how to go about things, but with my inner dragon's guidance, I will try my best to make it good for you." And because he couldn't help himself. "As to rough bed play, you might be surprised by what you end up craving. What your inner beast eventually desires."

It took almost more than he had to keep all the various things he wanted to do to her out of his mind. How she might groan and sob with pleasure because he would make that happen often. Many times a day, at the very least.

Based on the way she coughed nervously and took several more sips of ale, she was catching his desires anyway. If that weren't enough, the musky, sweet scent of her arousal had just hit his nostrils, and he couldn't help but inhale sharply. Could not keep from grunting in approval at how appealing it was to him. *She* was to him.

And that helped him see just how he should go about things.

He hated what she'd shared with him earlier about why she had yet to lose her virginity. Loathed that anyone had harmed her, if only with words. Had he been there, he would have cut their tongues out and fed them to the wolves. Had he been there years later, when men were equally cruel to her, their fates would have been far more brutal.

Yet he had not been there for any of it. Instead, he was here for how all those moments had made her feel. For the insecurities they left in their wake where none should exist. To that end, it seemed only right that he tore away all the harm others had done to her and help her see what he saw when he looked at her. Help her regain long-lost confidence.

"How do you like the ale?" he asked, already sensing its effect on her. It was offering more than just a calming effect.

"It's not too bad." She peeked into her mug and smiled at him in a way that made his chest tighten in an unusual way. "It seems I might be drinking it a bit too fast, though."

"No faster than I," he said softly, mesmerized by the way she looked in this light. Any light, for that matter. Therefore, rebuilding her confidence came effortlessly. "You are so much more beautiful than you realize, Athena." He set aside his cup and ran the pad of his thumb along her soft jawline. "Your skin...the way it looks...feels...."

He struggled to find the words, but he was no bard.

"It's my Greek ancestry," she stuttered, her voice a weak squeak. "And Italian...southern Italy, including Sicily but mostly Greece...but genetically, it *could* be the Italian because—"

Sensing a long, intricate explanation coming, he closed his mouth over hers and finally, at last, kissed her like men should have been kissing her all along. By the same token, he was relieved they hadn't because he might have sought them out and cut them down where they stood for kissing, let alone touching her. Setting aside Athena's stunning beauty, her mouth was so intensely alluring it was a wonder she hadn't been kissed properly before this. Then again, as he set aside her ale and cupped her cheek, he realized he'd never quite kissed like this either.

Not when her lips slowly melted beneath his, and kissing a woman became something altogether different than what it had been before. Hers wasn't the abrupt kiss of Åse or kisses women had tried to steal from him over the years, but another sort entirely. The exchange was deep and warm and arousing in a whole new way.

Especially when he slanted his mouth more firmly over hers and her lips opened to him. Accepted him. Because it was just that. An acceptance on her human's part that gave way to what quickly became a deep, passionate kiss. One that made them both groan before her tongue met his and everything intensified.

He wasn't sure when, but he pulled her onto his lap, chanted away her braids, and dug his hand into her thick, silky hair so he could lock her in place and taste more of her. Keep her. Because that's what it felt like as their tongues swirled and they kept kissing. Tasting. Becoming one in a way he didn't think possible with a simple kiss.

But then, kissing Athena wasn't simple. Not at all. Not when he felt the near unquenchable fire building in her. Dragon flames that had been held back for far too long. Repressed since the day she'd been born.

They burned beneath her human skin. Lusted in a way that did away with any insecurity and shyness she'd felt. Quickly made it clear as she rolled her backside on his engorged arousal that her inner dragon would take the intimacy of this moment away from her human half for the sheer pleasure of having her mate deep inside her.

A driving need seen clearly when she tried to straddle him while still kissing, but he didn't allow it. Her human half would have what it deserved after a lifetime of feeling undesirable, so he repositioned them until she was beneath him on the furs and kept kissing her. Kissed her until her inner dragon simmered down and let him have his way with her human half.

Although it was strange not seizing what a female willingly offered, he had made a promise he wouldn't take Athena's human half without her consent, so it was crucial her inner beast didn't take this moment from her. More than that, it was important she truly felt what she should have been feeling for years.

So he prayed to any god willing to listen to keep his inner beast tamed and touched her while kissing her. Lightly, gently, he ran his hand from her full breast to the indentation of her waist to the flare of her hip until he lifted her thigh just enough she felt his weight on her more securely.

So she felt the weight of his painfully hard cock.

In turn, she did the same, gripping the front of his tunic with one hand while the other hand wandered. Felt. Explored. From his shoulder to his back until she bravely slipped her hand beneath his tunic and ran it over his flesh.

Had he been any other man desperate for her, he might have shied away when she touched more imperfections and ridged scars than any twenty-first-century male would have, but he wasn't that sort. Even if females from his era saw them as hideous, he wouldn't care. Each and every one had been well-earned and made him the dragon he was today.

"I see them," she whispered against his lips, surprising him. "I see the battle behind every single one of them. The exceptional valor..."

She trailed off as she yanked at his tunic until he pulled it off and kept kissing her. He knew she wanted to see him, but he would only give her the choice to feel for now, and he made that clear telepathically. Then he made it clear physically when he kissed his way down her neck, slipped his hand into her pants, and found the moist folds between her luscious thighs.

When she tensed, he kissed her again and kept stroking her until she relaxed, groaned, and pushed back against him. Fascinated despite himself, he pulled back enough so he could enjoy watching her eyes roll back in her head and flutter shut. Relish how she arched into his touch and came to life beneath his fingertips.

Not giving her time to shrink back into her own self-doubt, he chanted away her tunic and feasted his eyes on her full, rounded breasts before he fondled one and pulled her taut, pebbled nipple into his mouth.

"Oh, God," she gasped and thrust her hips against him before she arched sharply and froze in wide-mouthed wonder before she quivered all over. He had never seen or felt anything like watching her peak, and it made his vision haze red.

Even though he was far, far more aroused than he could ever remember being, he'd never wanted to bring more of that unabashed pleasure out in another as he did Athena without being inside her. To ease her into everything she could possibly feel before she truly felt what it could be like with a man. A male dragon.

With *him*.

And he set to making that clear no matter what it took.

Chapter Thirteen

A THENA TRIED TO remain focused, *think*, but the moment Týr's mouth closed over hers, she was well and truly lost to coherent thought. She sensed he was trying to take things slow so this would be special for her, but her inner beast was in a pure frenzy, trying to surface and take over.

Yet still, somehow, he kept it under control.

And he did it effortlessly, making her explode all around him the moment his hands slipped into her pants, and he pulled a painfully sensitive nipple into his warm mouth. She couldn't explain the euphoria he'd catapulted her into, only that it was never-ending as he kept going, stroking her more, only to pull the other nipple into his mouth.

After that, everything became a blur of incredible sensations during which she was sometimes fully aware of what he did and, other times, lost in another climax. She had never felt anything like it, *him*, and the feelings he wrung from her seemed endless.

In fact, he made her feel so much, so worshiped for lack of a better word, she barely realized he had removed her clothes altogether. Hardly realized he had laid her bare for him until his hot tongue was swirling down her sensitive belly, he spread her thighs, and his mouth was where his fingers had been moments before.

"Ohhh," she moaned as he wrapped one large, strong hand around the side of her neck and the other over her hip, locking her in place. She gripped the fur beneath, held on tight, and tried to keep from cresting another peak, but it was too late, and she cried out, falling over the edge yet again.

"Týr," she tried to say, but the words were lost to her when he kissed her mouth again and resumed stroking between her thighs. This time, however, he pressed a finger deep inside her, and she shivered with a whole new type of awareness.

"It won't be long now, my fiery little mate," he murmured in her ear, repeating it in Norse. *"Brennende liten kompis."* He stretched her further with a second finger. "Do you understand? *Forstår du?"*

She understood and never wanted anything more. Whatever fear she'd suffered had long vanished beneath his touch, leaving her with an unexplainable ache even the best orgasm couldn't fill. One that made her desperate to feel every inch of him.

To be with him in a way that would be theirs and theirs alone.

"I understand," she whispered hoarsely, turning her mouth to his, hungry for his kisses. For how she lost all sense of reality and her whole body ignited in pure pleasure at the mere feel of his lips against hers.

A mouth and lips and tongue that delved deeper, drawing her into a kiss so mind-blowing she hardly realized his fingers were no longer pressing into her but something else.

"Shh, my little dragon," he whispered against her lips when she tensed. "I will not hurt you…never hurt you…."

With his gentle words came no hesitation but complete surrender, and she relaxed, allowing him to press deeper. She'd always thought there would be at least a pinch of pain when the time came, and more recently, quite a bit of it with a man his size, but there was none. Rather, as he stretched and filled her one easy inch at a time, she felt anything but pain.

Anything but poignant, tear-invoking pleasure.

She also felt the tremendous amount of patience he exercised by not taking her far more swiftly. How hard he fought the urge. Became as much a warrior against his own desires as he was against the many foes he'd fought over the years. In fact, he was so patient he stilled once he'd fully seated himself despite how difficult.

"Are you alright?" He cupped her cheek and searched her eyes. "Are you in pain?"

"No," she replied, her voice nothing more than a raspy, aroused whisper. "Pretty much the opposite."

And she soon learned it was only going to get better when he kissed her softly and moved, thrusting his hips slowly at first. So slow and deep that not just the exquisite sensation but the pure intimacy of it brought fresh tears to her eyes.

Yet she wanted more. Needed it with sudden urgency.

"Týr," she groaned and wrapped her legs around him, pulling him deeper still. So deep, she groaned even longer this time and urged him on. Wanted him to move faster. Take her where she sensed he could.

Based on how taut his muscles had become, he'd held back until now for her benefit. Yet it seemed the moment she pulled him even closer and urged him on, his patience snapped because he picked up the pace considerably.

Afire at the feel of him, she made more sounds than she knew she was capable of, from groans to moans to crying out and maybe even panting. How could she not when he pushed her higher and higher? So high she dug her nails into his sweat-slicked back and met his thrusts.

So high her vision hazed red with her inner beast.

"Not yet," he rasped in her ear. "Not this time."

Before she understood what he meant, he nipped the side of her neck and ground so deep she flew over the edge and belted out a long, strangled cry. Right there with her, he locked up inside her and released a ragged groan.

She was fairly certain she dug her nails in even deeper as the feeling of him throbbing inside her somehow heightened her climax. An orgasm crashed over her so intensely, she bit down hard on her lower lip, and her cry became more of a whimper.

She had no idea how long it went on, but it seemed blissfully unending as it gradually lessened in intensity and turned into a peaceful afterglow of drowsy ebbing and flowing pleasure. It also made her limbs useless as he rolled them into a sitting position without losing contact and had her straddle him. Well, more like draped her against him with her cheek resting on his shoulder because nothing seemed to work except for where she continued pulsing around him.

All the while, he stroked her hair and rubbed her back, sometimes massaging low enough that he grazed her backside, keeping her orgasm going at a low simmer. She wouldn't have thought a man like him could have been capable of such tenderness, and it warmed her heart, burrowing into a place inside her she hardly recognized. A place she wasn't sure she was ready to acknowledge with someone she had only just met.

"Yet we did not just meet," he rumbled, the vibration of his deep voice pleasurable against her sensitive breasts. "Not nearly, and we both know it."

She supposed she did. More so by the hour. By the very minute.

"What did you mean when you said not this time?" she murmured once she at last found her voice. When she went to sit back, she realized she'd dug her nails in his back far too deeply and had to have drawn blood. She looked at him with concern. "Did I hurt you?"

She started to get up so she could see just how bad it was, but he bent his knees and kept her locked in place.

"I find the kind of pain you inflicted pleasurable, Athena." He cupped the side of her neck and met her eyes. "Especially pleasurable coming from you." The corner of his mouth curled up in a roguish smile. "I will wear every wound with which you mark me with pride, *brennende liten kompis.*"

She warmed at the nickname he'd given her. "Even so, probably best that I not make a habit of hurting you."

"Why when I wish you would?" He ran his fingertip over her nails. "With these." Then he rubbed the pad of his thumb over her lower lip, implying her teeth. "And with these." He grazed his knuckles alongside her eyes. "Because these told me you enjoyed it every bit as much as me."

"That's what you meant when you said not this time," she said, finally understanding. "You didn't want my dragon surfacing any more than it already had." Her eyes rounded at what that might imply. "Could it shift me against my will while we're...well, you know."

"No." Definitely more lighthearted since making love, he chuckled. "That might prove more than a little awkward for my human half. Your inner beast can, however, surface quite a bit within your human and make you crave the roughness I spoke of before." He shook his head. "And I didn't want that for you your first time."

"I see." Even though she didn't. Not really. If anything, she was eager to explore where it had wanted to take her. Acutely aware he was hard inside her again, she dusted her fingers over each angry scar on his chest. "What about the second time?"

Interest flared in his eyes, and his brows swept up. "Already?"

"Isn't that why you kept me here?" she said softly, surprised by how sultry she could sound when she shifted her hips ever so slightly, reminding him of their current position. Then again, everything she'd just experienced with him had bolstered her confidence. How she had made him feel despite being so inexperienced.

"I kept you here because I didn't want to let you go just yet," he said gruffly, clearly aroused by her. *Taken* by her. She felt it in the way he kept touching her here and there as if mapping her out. Memorizing her. "Dragons might heal quickly, but I still don't want to risk you being sore tomorrow or lacking rest."

"A tomorrow that might mean our end," she reminded, hating to say it. "*Your* end."

Not tired in the least, she listened to her inner dragon and rolled her hips just enough to tease him. A low growl of approval rumbled deep in his chest, and his member leapt inside her, arousing her to no end.

"I don't want to sleep right now," she whispered as fire seemed to roll beneath her skin. Beautiful, mesmerizing flames fueled by the hungry look in his eyes. By a cock that grew more and more rigid, if possible. "Besides, aren't you at your best when well-satisfied?" She trailed her fingers over his ripped abs. "So it stands to reason you would fight better tomorrow if we don't go to sleep just yet, right?"

"Considering I don't think your inner dragon has any intention of doing otherwise," he grunted, his breathing switching when she rolled her hips again, "I cannot see how I have much choice."

Where some might hear that as unflattering resolve, his true feelings came through not just in his thoughts but also in his actions. How he continued to look at her. Visually devour her every bit as much as she did him. And his thoughts were just as much, if not more arousing, from how beautiful he found every inch of her to how good she made him feel just by being close.

Then, of course, he liked the small movements she made with her hips.

"Take your pleasure, *brennende liten kompis*." He rested his head back against the rock wall and watched her from beneath half-mast lids. "Learn what brings both sides of you pleasure."

He brought both sides pleasure. Every last part of him. But she understood what he meant. He wanted her to take charge. Get used to her own body in ways she never had before.

So she did, feeling hardly any shyness at all now.

How could she when she rolled her hips again, only deeper this time, and a fresh burst of pleasure fanned everywhere? When his pupils flared in approval, and his muscles flexed as if he barely held himself back?

Loving how good he felt and eager to see how much pleasure she could bring them both, she braced her hands on his broad shoulders and ground her hips back and forth while rolling them. The more she did it, the more she struggled for breath, and fire once again felt like it sizzled beneath her skin.

Flames so intense her vision hazed red once more.

This time, he didn't slow her inner beast from surfacing but let her have her way with him. And did she ever, finding a rhythm that seemed to please both of them a great deal because that same low growl started in his chest again before his eyes flared with his inner dragon.

Days ago, that would have terrified her, but not now. Instead, her vision hazed even redder, and everything inside came alive in a whole new way. Near painful pleasure made her dig her nails into his shoulders and ride him even faster. Harder as she moved up and down, grinding her hips until his eyes flamed brighter, and she knew he wouldn't be able to hold back much longer. She was stripping away his willpower until she owned his strong body.

And that was the best aphrodisiac she had ever felt.

It was a strange possessive feeling that had everything to do with them being mates. With the ferocious give and take that came from finding each other once again.

Because they *had* found one another again.

She was certain of it.

And that only fueled her driving need to pull him deeper into her until he couldn't say no if he tried. Could not stop from giving her everything her body, her very soul, needed. So she rode him even faster until she dug her nails into one shoulder, nipped the side of his neck hard, and took him as intensely as he'd taken her before.

This time, clearly pushed to his limit, he grabbed her ass hard, slammed up into her, and roared his release. Aroused to her breaking point by his primal, raw response, she sailed over the edge especially hard. So hard her vision, along with her body, seemed to explode with fire and heat and so much pleasure it speared through her in sharp, aching, *perfect* waves.

Waves that must have lured her to sleep or even made her pass out because the next thing she knew, she was curled up next to Týr under the furs, and he was sound asleep. Something had woken her, though, hadn't it? Seconds later, she heard Quinn clearly in her mind despite the centuries between them.

"Run, Athena!" she yelled, terrified for her. *"Run, or you'll all die!"*

Caught somewhere between a dream state and reality, she didn't pause to question her friend's request but bolted, shifting to dragon form effortlessly. She raced through the tunnel, her magic able to fit her beast wherever it needed to go.

As she ran, she sensed something dark and sinister closing in on her at an alarming speed. A magical presence determined to stop her. Worse still, kill her. She felt its malicious intent. Smelled its stink merging with sulfur and methane gases as she raced into the far more dangerous chambers of the mud volcano.

She needed to stay one step ahead of it.

Him.

She had to save everyone, just as Quinn had said.

For a second, she thought she saw a tiny blue dragon ahead of her, showing her where to go, but the next moment, it was gone. Vanished in the murky, lethal gasses of pure hell before everything crashed down around her, and she knew it was too late.

Far, far too late.

.

Chapter Fourteen

THE MOMENT ATHENA bolted upright and flew out of the cave, Týr snapped awake and raced after her, warning Rafe and Åse they had best follow because she was moving fast.

Terrifyingly fast.

Her dragon had found great strength from the intimacy they had shared last night, and it showed with her confident, fluid movements. Actions he realized she was not fully in control of because when he roared for her to stop, her mind was distant. Somewhere else.

"Haunted," Rafe said telepathically, just as upset. *"Something dangerous pursues her...something from this era but from another all at once."*

"What does that mean?" he growled, sensing Rafe and Åse right on his tail, flying into what could be mortal danger alongside him. *"Do not follow. Go back. She's heading straight into the volcano. Straight into..."*

He couldn't get the rest of his telepathic words out when he caught up with Athena, only to find her flailing around in a noxious mud pocket she should have been able to easily break free from. Instead, she was quickly smothering to death in the murky dank substance.

"No," he roared, crashing into her and the cloying substance so hard he dislodged her with a loud pop. When that happened, she flailed again, but this time as if trying to shake free of whatever had gripped her.

"What happened?" she exclaimed, sounding discombobulated. *"Where am I?"*

"Nowhere you want to be." Rafe whipped past them. *"Follow me and fly like you've never flown before or else…"*

There was no need to say more. Everyone sensed the impending eruption and raced after Rafe. Týr tried to put the females ahead of him, but Åse being Åse, managed to situate herself behind him, taking up the rear defensive position.

"Go!" Åse roared when he tried to take the rear again, only to struggle the moment he wasn't close to Athena. Struggle when his dragon felt he wasn't near enough to keep its mate safe.

So, unfortunately, all he could do was keep on Athena's tail and protect her the best he could. Pray to the gods they saw everyone out safely. Especially Åse, because she was the most vulnerable as Midgard's underbelly roared toward them with all her might. An overheated deathtrap that would kill all four if they didn't get out now.

"It's fire," Athena exclaimed, her inner scientist pushing past her confusion. *"It should only be gasses, not flames, in this location."*

Whatever it was, they were running out of time based on the sheer speed Rafe was going and the urgency he felt. Fast, faster, until his cousin roared, *"Now swim with everything in you! All the magic you can muster!"*

A blink later, Rafe crashed through a weakening in the rocky surface, and they pushed against a rush of seawater. Despite Týr fearing for Åse, his inner beast was even more terrified for Athena as they swam upward against the sheer force and pressure of the heavy ocean bearing down on them. It seemed Athena's dragon truly had grown stronger because she held her own and raced upward as fire exploded in a long, hot fissure beneath them.

"Are you behind me, Åse?" he growled when he couldn't feel her presence. *"Tell me you are behind me."*

Moments later, he shot up out of the sea behind Rafe and Athena only to find King Knud's ship, of all things, waiting for them.

"Shift and land on my boat," the former enemy king roared into their minds. *"Or lose your lives here and now to great magic."*

"He's right." Rafe shifted and landed, choosing their enemy over whatever this was without realizing Ulrik had struck a private alliance with Knud. That, in itself, said much about what roared up behind them, and Rafe confirmed it. *"The fire following us is unnatural."*

Right behind Rafe, Athena shifted and landed safely, followed by Týr.

"Where is Åse?" He scanned the ship of wary crewmen but saw no sign of her.

"There," Athena gasped, coughing smoke as she staggered and fell against Knud, who held her upright. "She's right there," Athena managed hoarsely, finally dragging in air. She seemed able to see what they couldn't. Fearful, her eyes met Týr's. "Just ahead of it…"

Half a breath later, Åse shot out of the water seconds before a burp of rancid ocean spewed upward, giving her no choice but to shift midair too soon as she lunged at the boat. Certain she would die a horrible death if she landed anywhere but on the ship, Týr raced to the edge and grabbed her hand before she hit the water, only for Rafe to grab the back of his tunic before he went over, too.

"I've got you," Rafe grunted. He pulled Týr back, and, in turn, Týr yanked Åse into the ship before a plume of fire burst out of the water and shot toward the sky.

"Oars up," Knud roared and filled the sails with dragon magic, lurching the ship away from the dangerous, boiling sea just in the nick of time.

Meanwhile, Týr fell to his knees when Åse did and held onto her as she coughed twice as much thick, black smoke as Athena had. If that weren't alarming enough, smoke poured off her as though her skin was seconds from igniting in flames before, after what seemed far too many minutes, it finally eased up.

"Are you alright?" Still kneeling in front of her, he cupped the side of Åse's neck when her coughing subsided, and she began dragging in air. He searched her eyes. "Are you well, Åse? Talk to me."

He was surprised when he saw her eyes moisten for a flicker of a moment. A moment too long for Åse because she'd never, not once, shown that kind of emotion in front of others, let alone enemy warriors.

"Here." He held a skin of water to her lips when Knud handed it to him. "Drink first."

She took several small, tentative sips before she snatched it from him and drank greedily, downing it in several long swigs before wiping her mouth with the back of her hand and resting her forehead against his shoulder for a moment to regain her strength.

Finally, at last, she spoke, and it wasn't good.

"I have said it from the beginning, and I will say it again," she ground out before she raised her head, speaking loud enough for all to hear. "She *will* be the death of you, my friend." She narrowed her eyes at Athena, blaming her for what just happened. Åse clearly cared nothing for the mortal danger in which she herself had been put, but Týr subjected to such danger was another story. "Do you hear me, *svak en?*" Her dragon eyes flared in disgust, and she seethed, "You are *not* Valkyrie, but will be the death of him, weak one!"

"Actually," Rafe clarified, resting a supportive hand on Åse's shoulder because kin should always come first. "If not for her waking us, we would have all been dead right now. Whatever that was—"

"Is the least of your worries if my sons spy you on this ship," Knud groused. He scanned the horizon and eyed Rafe warily, clearly unconvinced he could be trusted. In turn, Rafe eyed him with equal distrust despite Týr telepathically catching him up on the truce.

But then it was a truce that didn't include Zane *or* Rafe.

Knud gestured at the animal skins covering a section of the ship for long travels. "Take cover until we are further north because this eruption will draw much attention, and none of it good."

"Is my king well?" Týr asked, worried about how peace talks went with the dragon prince.

"*Ja.*" Knud's grim expression said it all. "As expected, he gained no ground with Magnus, so he returned to defend your kingdoms with his Valkyrie."

"You mean his queen," Týr made clear how Keira should be addressed whether Knud chose to recognize Ulrik as King of Norway or not. "*Our* queen."

Knud merely nodded once and said nothing.

Confident Åse was well enough now, Týr couldn't help but pull Athena into his arms the moment they were under cover. Could not help but hold her close and will away the terror that still simmered inside him and his beast at how close they had come to losing her.

Because it had been terrifyingly close.

"I'm okay," Athena said, her voice choppy as he pulled her onto his lap and wrapped his fur cloak around them, even though she already wore one. "I am...truly..."

She might say she was okay in an attempt to remain strong, but he felt her body trembling in shock. Her very soul. Whatever was down there had rocked her to her core every bit as much as the rest of them.

"I know you are." He rested her cheek against his chest and wrapped his fur more securely around her, hiding her from judgmental eyes when she sobbed softly.

"This was not your fault, Athena," he said into her mind, wrapping her up more tightly in his arms. *"Rafe said you saved us, and I do not doubt it. Not for a moment."*

How could he when Athena meant a great deal to him in so little time? When he knew she had a good heart? And he knew that because of how intensely they had bonded last night. Having her in his arms, either like this or straddling him in the heat of passion, was like nothing he'd ever felt before.

Laying with a woman was second nature to him, done so often, it had become regimental in a way to keep his inner Helheim stable. Yet spreading Athena's quivering thighs and pressing deep inside her had felt anything but routine. Anything but stabilizing. Instead, it felt like coming home merged with the best sensual experience of his life. Like everything that had been so level and dependable had been turned upside down in the best way possible.

"I didn't save you, though," Athena eventually murmured aloud and looked at him. "Týr, as far as I remember, Quinn saved us." She closed her eyes as if gathering herself for what she needed to say and finally looked at Åse, who was sharpening her blade across from them because that's what she did when she needed to regain control. "And you're right, Åse. I did, *do*, put Týr's life at risk just by being here. I'm certain of it." She shook her head. "But you have to believe it's not intentional." She pressed her lips together for a moment, fighting emotion. "Never, ever, intentional."

"Why should I believe that?" Åse bit out, frowning as she gestured loosely at the smoldering, smoking sea falling further behind them. "Why when—"

"Because I love him," Athena said softly, vehemently, before her gaze narrowed from the simmering ocean to Knud to what lay ahead, clearly caught by something. "Where are we going?" She swallowed hard in alarm and looked at their former enemy despite having never been introduced to him. "Where are you taking us?"

While Týr would much rather focus on what she'd just said in regards to loving him, his inner beast was more concerned by her alarm. With both the curiosity and fear roiling inside her.

"King Ulrik said I would find you on the sea near the border betwixt my land and Magnus's, amid pure terror, and so I did." King Knud eyed Athena with too much uncertainty for Týr's taste. "He also said, as per our discreet peace treaty, if I brought you to Frigid Peak, it would aid in our cause. He believes it will bring us one step closer to finding true peace betwixt our kingdoms and ensuring the safety of dragonkind on Midgard."

141

"And he is not wrong." Rafe continued to keep as wary an eye on Knud as the enemy king did him. "Athena said yesterday that there is much to find on what we call Frigid Peak but will someday be known as the Isle of Jan Mayen. A truth we need to heed."

She hadn't quite said that, but Týr got the sense someone had besides Ulrik, and it seemed Athena knew who.

"I might have implied it but was never insistent about it," Athena said softly, looking closer at Rafe. "You've heard from Quinn too, haven't you?"

It almost seemed for a too-heavy moment that Rafe fought telling her the truth, but something about the way the wind filled the sail beyond Knud's magic, and they flew over the darkening waves even faster made Rafe take pause. Made whatever existed inside him beyond what his kin understood heighten with a strange sense of anticipation mixed with trepidation.

"Quinn woke you, Athena, and in turn, you saved us." When Rafe looked from Týr to Åse, his eyes shimmered the same blue-black as the sea behind him. "Know that and know it well, cousin. Quinn might have led Athena into the chambers that nearly ended us, but it was Athena, *always* Athena, who showed the truest courage. Who would have died for you a thousand times over."

While Týr agreed that was undoubtedly at the root of who Athena was, whether she realized it or not, he got the strange sense Rafe saw beyond the obvious. That he was aware of something that might have happened to Athena in another life, which had very likely been Týr's previous life, too.

"I saw only Týr's courage when he saved Athena from certain death," Åse said, clearly unsoftened by Athena's declaration of love for him. But then, as his mother would phrase it, actions spoke louder than words for Åse. To her stubborn mind, Athena was a threat to his life, and she remained unwilling to see past that.

"Even so." Rafe gave Athena a look of reassurance before gazing northwest. "She is very courageous, and it will only be a matter of time before we see proof of that."

"What did Quinn say to you?" Athena asked. "Did she tell you how she knew we were in danger back there? What we might expect at—"

"No," Rafe said, clearly done talking about it. "Nothing other than we must go to Frigid Peak."

"He's lying," Athena said into Týr's mind. *"Why, though? Wouldn't giving us as much information as possible when going into another dangerous place be beneficial?"*

"It would," he agreed. *"But that doesn't mean Rafe will share right away, if at all. Because of the distrust and dissent he deals with due to his Celtic magic, he tends, as a rule, to say things only if necessary when it's often clear he knows more. He's been like that since we were boys."*

"So it's a bit of a defense mechanism on his part," Athena surmised, considering his cousin. *"Although I get the distinct impression it's a means to keep others safe too."*

"You're embracing your inner dragon and, in turn, your magic indeed," he noted. *"Because few care about others like Rafe does without getting recognition for it, outside of his own people, of course."*

"What about those at your Lair and Ulrik's Fortress?" she wondered.

"Many do, but not all." He sighed. *"Though the Great War between the Norse and Celtic gods is a generation behind us, some still distrust the Celts."*

"That sounds like a lonely existence for Rafe."

"It is because he generally stays away these days, so we don't have to deal with dissent amongst our people."

"Even though you and Ulrik surely wouldn't allow it?" she assumed, and she was correct.

"Ja." He shook his head. *"But dissent is not always out in the open. Rather, it festers in darkened corners more so than ever these days."*

"Which could lead to bigger problems before you ever see them coming," she deduced, about to go on when she seemed to sense something and left his lap.

"What is it?" he asked aloud, staying close to her on a ship with so many male dragons. Thankfully, she was no longer a virgin, but still. She was female and fertile.

"I don't know..." She squinted against the cold wind and peered northwest. "I just got this overwhelming feeling..."

He pulled her back against him and wrapped an arm around her waist to keep her stable. "Of what?"

"Of that," she whispered, her inner beast suddenly on high alert as Frigid Peak appeared on the distant horizon. "It doesn't look at all how my dragon thinks it should."

Chapter Fifteen

A STRANGE SHIVER rippled through Athena when the volcano known as Beerenberg appeared on the horizon in all her glacial glory, shimmering in dappled sunlight against a backdrop of sinister black storm clouds.

"What do you mean it doesn't look right?" Týr rumbled against her back, making her as aware of him and the strong arm he had wrapped around her waist as she was of the dangerous Arctic island looming in the distance. Far more aware of him than she should have been, given the terror they had experienced at the last volcano.

It was strange gauging everything by numbers and charts, graphs, samples, and experiments for the better part of her life, only to experience something beyond scientific rationalization when it came to Týr. What they shared went beyond mere chemistry to something soul-deep, perhaps even theological, and that wasn't where scientists usually dwelled. Yet here she was caught up in something that defied logical explanation when she knew, without a doubt, the island of Jan Mayan hadn't always looked the way it did now, and that could only mean one thing.

She had been here before in a previous life.

"What did it look like?" Týr asked, following her thoughts enough to understand what she'd just realized.

"Like more," she said softly. Her words came out in foggy puffs as she wrapped her fur cloak tighter against ever-dropping temperatures and biting wind. "I just can't see what that *more* is." She shook her head. "All I know is there was more to that island. More than just a seven thousand, four hundred seventy-foot-tall stratovolcano dominating the northeastern end of Nord-Jan."

"So you have been here before," he said, understanding what she insinuated. "Your dragon has been here in another life."

"Yes, I'm certain of it." She rested her arm over his, grateful he was close. Never so thankful he'd saved her life from the pure terror she'd felt below the mud volcano. "Though I never visited it in the twenty-first century, I studied it enough to know its appearance is unchanged between our eras." She took in its icy grandeur and shook her head in disbelief. "I wanted to come here a few times in college because it was unique being the northernmost active volcano in the world, but something always got in the way." She shrugged. "Then, once I graduated and got a job, one big project after another kept me busy elsewhere."

"And now you think there is more to that," he said. "That it wasn't coincidental that you didn't get here sooner."

"I do." She glanced over her shoulder into his deep blue eyes and almost wished she hadn't because it instantly aroused her, and now wasn't the time for that. "What if whoever tried to lure me into the mud volcano somehow influenced me back home? Influenced me despite over a thousand years between us?"

"What do you mean, *lured* you?" Alarmed, Týr frowned, turned her until he held her close again, and tilted her chin so her eyes stayed with his. "Whatever was down there didn't try to *lure* you but chased you and tried to *kill* you, Athena."

"Maybe," she murmured, trying to wrap her mind around what precisely had happened, but her memories suddenly felt scattered and undependable. "I'm not sure that was his ultimate goal, though. If anything, I think he was trying to remind me of something so he could...pull me closer somehow."

"*He?*" Týr's brows lowered sharply, and a fierce scowl settled on his face. "As you heard, and as you damn well saw and felt once you were clear of that mud trap, what we encountered down there was powerful dark magic bordering on evil." He shook his head. "And it meant to end you, mate. I saw it and felt it and did not allow it. Would *never* allow it if it were the last thing I did."

Before she could reply, he went on. "This happened when I could not feel you in my mind, didn't it? This connection you shared with the enemy?"

"I don't know." She rested her hand against his chest and sighed. "All I know is the relief I felt when you saved me. It was like waking up from a nightmare. Knowing you were there was—"

Before she could finish her sentence, he tilted her chin up again and brushed his lips across hers once, twice, before closing his mouth more firmly over hers, letting her know with a kiss that he would always be there. Always save her as long as he was breathing, then quite possibly from the other side in Helheim itself.

She could hardly believe she'd confessed aloud to loving him earlier but was glad she had because she meant it. Understood it in ways science disallowed after bonding with him so deeply the night before. He hadn't said it in return yet, but he didn't need to. She felt it inside him, from his dragon to his human.

No testing necessary. No experiments needed.

"We can only get the ship so close to shore," Knud said, interrupting the moment and good thing. If she kept on like this, she might tear Týr's clothes off and take him right there for all to see. So said the incredible fire filling her blood at his kiss. At being so close to him.

He released a deep rumble in his chest that told her he approved of her thoughts before slowly pulling his mouth away and eyeing the island, which wasn't far off now.

"Bring us as close to the southern side as you can," Týr said. "We will walk from there."

Athena nodded in agreement because the elongated, somewhat flat southern end of the isle known as Sör-Jan would be easier to come ashore than the northern side. At one time, Sör-Jan had consisted of a Holocene rifting fissure volcano system comprised of splatter cones that likely erupted in short bursts running the length of the island, reaching far south under the sea, but now all was quiet and dormant.

"Why not shift into our dragons?" she wondered. "It would be easier to withstand the frigid climate if we did."

"Because of what transpired at the mud volcano," Týr reminded. "Its fire and the magic associated with it will draw dragons far and wide like a moth to a flame. When that happens, there's every chance they will trail us if you're associated with the fire in some way we've yet to understand." He shrugged a shoulder as he chanted her into a thicker fur cloak with a heavy hood that wrapped around and covered her face against the harsh elements. "Then there's always the natural attraction dragons have to seismic activity and volcanic eruptions in general."

She didn't know about that. "Really?"

"Really," he said. "So even though you're drawn to volcanoes more than most, they possess a natural allure to our kind, no matter how deadly they might be."

"Duly noted." Somehow, that made her feel better about her addiction. "You might have mentioned that when you knew how fire-hungry I am...was."

Because, yet again, she realized that was waning. Especially since being with him last night. It was almost as if the fiery pleasure she'd found in his arms filled that fire-craving void in her life with something just as combustible and addictive.

"Then I will be sure to feed your addiction often," he murmured, catching her thoughts. A small, knowing smile curled his mouth, and an arousing flicker of teasing fire flickered in his pointed gaze. "As I hope you will feed mine."

Had someone told her days ago she'd be more than willing to become a male dragon's sex slave to keep him in a good mood, she would have called them crazy, but now she looked forward to the lusty chore.

"Sex slave?" he said huskily enough to let her know that aroused him before he chuckled and made light of it, clearly trying to tame an untimely erection. "You are ambitious, *brennende liten kompis.*" Obviously unable to help himself, he leaned close and murmured in her ear, "Yet I do so appreciate ambition, my fiery little mate, so I will hold you to your lusty chore once this is all over."

"I wish you much luck with that, friend," Åse said, joining them, more aware of their exchange than Athena would like her to be. The Viking woman narrowed her eyes at the daunting mountain in the distance. "As is, we have much to face betwixt then and now, and I fear it will put you in even more danger if your mate has anything to say about it."

"Well, at least she can admit I'm your mate now," Athena muttered, manifesting gloves and heavier boots with better traction. She understood Åse's behavior earlier because she was all about keeping Týr safe, too, but it was getting old. Athena hadn't intentionally put him in harm's way, so she refused to keep feeling guilty about it.

"Because I *am* his mate, Åse," Athena went on, empowered by the changes embracing her inner dragon had on her. The confidence and clarity it lent. "And, as I said before, I *do* love him. Every bit, if not more than you do."

Before Åse could respond with some snarky comeback, Athena joined King Knud and eyed the small boat he'd manifested to bring them ashore. "Thank you, King Knud." She knew enough about Keira's story to know the forty-something bearded blond king had been good to her. Then, good again, not to mention courageous, when he'd brought his men so close to the magically erupting mud volcano to save Athena and the others. "For everything."

"Might it lead us to better days." His wary gaze flickered from Rafe, who stood near the ship's helm eyeing the volcano, back to her. "Be careful, Mate to Týr, for the untrustworthy are all around us."

"Just because Rafe possesses Celtic magic doesn't mean he can't be trusted," she said. "It just means—"

"Celtic magic is the least of what he possesses," Knud grunted, frowning at her when he must have seen her confusion. "Have you not been told Rafe's powers are much more than a bit of foreign magic? What runs in his blood is a new type of magic born of Celtic and Norse godliness. A magic born of warring enemies."

He rested his hand on the hilt of the blade sheathed at his waist and glared at Rafe before looking her in the eyes, his warning chilling. "No Viking can be half dragon, half dark wizard, and not know far more than everyone else. Not know the end of a story before it has already begun. It is a far greater power than even the most powerful have if they but open their eyes and see what could be, *has* to be, a very real threat to us all."

"You should go no closer," Rafe said, glancing at them in a way that told her he'd likely overheard every discreet word Knud had uttered. He pointed at a less rocky portion of the shoreline. "We will go ashore there."

"Agreed," Týr said, lowering his head to Knud briefly enough to be respectful of his rank. He didn't have to, considering he and Knud were of the same rank, answerable only to Ulrik. Then, again proving he was his king's advocate always, Týr held out his hand to his former enemy. "I thank you for remaining true to your pact with my king and for saving me and my kin in our time of need. It will not be forgotten."

Knud caught his arm, hand to elbow, and briefly lowered his head as well, acknowledging he saw him as an equal. "Farewell, King Týr. May you discover what your king hopes you will on your journey."

Åse nodded to Knud as well, giving him the respect and thanks due him before they climbed down into the small boat. As expected, words weren't exchanged between Rafe and Knud, and Athena worried about that.

"*Yet you do not worry about Knud's warning,*" Týr said telepathically, his words a statement rather than a question as they started rowing for shore. "*You don't worry Rafe might be our greatest enemy without any of us seeing it.*"

"Not really. Not yet," she replied honestly, hoping it wasn't the case if for no other reason than the connection she suspected Rafe was making with Quinn. *"All I know is the more you Vikings stick together, the better. Moreover, the fewer enemies, the better. Four kingdoms against two beats the alternative."*

She felt his surprise at that because she referred to Ulrik's Fortress, Týr's Lair, Knud's Kingdom, and Rafe's Stronghold, against Zane's Keep and Knud's son, the dragon prince, not to mention his other son, Jørn, yet another unknown factor in all this but rumored to have once been in love with Rune.

"Even though you haven't met him yet, you think Zane guilty?" Týr asked. *"You think he will turn on Ulrik in the end if he hasn't already?"*

"As you well know, it's unwise to rule out anything." She wasn't entirely sure why she thought that either when she had yet to the meet the man, but she did.

Whatever was happening here in tenth-century Norway, Zane shouldn't be taken lightly, and that became evident soon thereafter.

Chapter Sixteen

THEY HAD JUST reached the rocky shores of Sør-Jan when Týr sensed the last person he wanted to. He glanced back at Knud's ship in alarm only to find it gone, much to his relief, considering Zane and two of his fellow dragons had just appeared on the horizon.

Rafe cursed under his breath and eyed the sky with disgust. "I will scout ahead and return swiftly if he proves every inch the enemy, I think him. Otherwise, I might cut him down where he stands."

Before anyone could reply, he vanished with a chant.

Athena narrowed her eyes at the incoming dragons and became just as tense, clearly recognizing his kin through Týr's mind's eye. "Why is he here?"

"Impossible to know with Zane," Týr muttered. "But best we assume Rafe's right and tread carefully."

Týr and Åse stepped closer to Athena in defensive positions with their hands on the hilts of their sheathed blades as Zane

153

landed and shifted, only for his second and third commands to continue circling overhead.

"What are you doing here?" Týr ground out, skipping formalities. He could only hope the better side of his cousin was surfaced right now.

"What do you think I'm doing here?" Zane rumbled. His fiery gaze roamed over Athena with appreciation. "When this lovely little female has managed to stir up dragons far and wide." A slow grin curled his mouth. "Which means she'll need more protection than the likes of you three could ever offer her."

"I can protect my mate without your help," Týr bit back. "So leave."

"Your *mate?*" Zane drawled, still eyeing Athena like she was a tasty bit of meat he wanted to sample. "Are you so sure, cousin?"

"He is," Athena said, her voice predictably shaky at first, given Zane's fierce appearance, including multiple piercings and more tattoos than the lot of them, not to mention the shaved slashes in his eyebrow signifying his high rank. "Zane, I assume?"

"You assume correctly, Athena."

When he stepped closer, Athena clearly surprised his cousin when she grabbed a blade from Åse in the blink of an eye and held it up in warning. "Stop right there." Her dragon eyes flared, and she shook her head. "Don't step any closer." Her gaze never wavered. "Because Týr *is* my mate, and my inner dragon won't hesitate to make that clear."

Even though Týr kept a scowl firmly in place for Zane's benefit, his inner dragon preened because of her possessive declaration and because he was proud of her courage.

Zane generally came off as too vicious and intimidating to tenth-century Midgard dragons with his imposing tribal appearance, so he was bound to be even more intimidating to a female from the future, but Athena held her ground. Then again, it seemed they had the better half of Zane at the moment.

Undaunted by Athena's veiled threat or the blade in her hand, the corner of his cousin's mouth twitched in amusement. "I would like nothing more than to see your inner beast try to defend Týr against me, fiery one." He shrugged and stepped back. "But alas, I have been sent to protect you." His cousin gestured in the direction of the mainland and kept grinning, clearly hoping trouble would find them. "Which, as it happens, are more enemy dragons than you're probably comfortable with." His flippant gaze flickered between Týr and Åse. "Considering you've but these two and a Celt protecting you." His brows swept up as he looked around. "Ah, but then, as usual, Rafe's scurried off, so maybe you only have these two."

"Who sent you?" Åse bit out, unconvinced Zane was here for anything more than to serve his own agenda.

"Our king, of course." He shrugged a shoulder. "As I'm sure you heard, and as to be expected, negotiations failed with the traitorous dragon prince, not to mention all are astir over the mud volcano, so I'm here to help." He glanced at his circling commanders. "*We're* here to help."

"Only two others, then?" Týr said, uneasy, because Zane's numerous dragons tended to trail after him wherever he went, and they counted far more than two. Worse yet, they were mostly Ancient and Múspellsheimr dragons, who were more ferocious sorts by half. So if they showed up and Zane really was the unknown enemy within their ranks, then Týr, Åse, and Rafe would be far outnumbered on this remote isle.

"Yet I don't sense large masses of enemy dragons heading this way," Athena said softly, absently even. Her gaze wandered over the snowy area surrounding them. "Somehow, this place is masking us...me..." Her eyes narrowed on Zane again. "Which begs the question...how did you know we were here?"

"King Ulrik said this would likely be the next place on your quest," Zane replied steadily enough to almost sound authentic. "And it seems he was right." His knowing gaze went from the looming mountain to her. "Although I'm surprised to find you on this side of the isle when you crave the other so much."

More and more distracted by their surroundings, Athena offered no response to that. Rather, various daunting emotions had begun churning inside her that had nothing to do with Zane and his possible threat. Emotions Týr felt just as strongly. So strongly they might have once been his own.

"I don't like it here, Týr," Athena said telepathically. "There's a terrible sadness. A catastrophic sense of loss." She shook her head. "Nothing is how it's supposed to be...how it was..." Her gaze lingered on the volcano in the distance. "We've got to head that way. Something's there we need to discover."

"My shield?" he assumed.

"I don't know," she murmured. "Hopefully."

He tried to reach out to Ulrik telepathically to confirm he'd sent Zane here, but the magical interference left over from the mud volcano eruption made it impossible. So he had no choice but to trust the last person he was inclined to trust because he knew his cousin wouldn't leave either way.

He could, however, try to keep him at a distance.

"We're heading into the mountain, Zane," he said. "If you truly are here at Ulrik's bequest, then we'll need you and your dragons to protect us from out here." He shook his head. "Rafe is the only one who can keep us safe inside the volcano, and I won't have you two battling each other in such a dangerous place."

"Why when Zane will be so weakened?" Rafe reminded Týr telepathically. *"He might be able to withstand the elements better than most with his Múspellsheimr blood, but the volcano will still drain his strength."*

He didn't need to ask to understand what his cousin implied.

Not only would it be an opportunity to find out if Zane was their hidden enemy, but a chance to end him. While he mostly agreed with Rafe's way of thinking, a small part of him remembered better days with Zane, and while he didn't trust him, he still cared for his brethren. On top of that, even if they did garner evidence of Zane's guilt, Ulrik would never forgive them for ending him without his permission. Without first being able to look him in the eye so he could understand why Zane had betrayed them in the first place.

"Although I think you would be safer with us closer—" Zane nodded once in acceptance of Týr's request— "my dragons and I will keep watch outside the mountain."

Týr nodded once in return, and the three started making their way across the craggy snow-swept landscape toward the looming monolith.

"He's not to be trusted," Åse growled once they left Zane behind. "For all we know, his entire kingdom could descend on us at any moment." She shook her head. "We would never stand a chance."

"On that, we agree," Rafe said, rejoining them. "Yet I get the distinct impression he bides his time for even richer rewards than slaying us and taking Athena. He wants to know what we discover here."

Although he seemed level enough, Týr could tell by the dark shadows fluctuating around his wizardly cousin that Rafe was in a foul mood. A bloodthirsty mood if he didn't know better. No doubt, his Celtic cousin wasn't a fan of being called a coward by Zane, of all people. A coward, despite his absence having kept things from escalating between them and strife breaking out that they didn't need right now.

"What would Zane want with me?" Athena said. "Even on the crazy chance I'm a Valkyrie, too, I can't imagine being here to protect anyone but Týr, which would make me pretty useless to him."

"Females, especially fertile ones are in high demand in these parts," Týr reminded, fighting rage at the mere thought of Zane and his minions getting their hands on her. "And given how you snatched that blade from Åse back there, not to mention your speed with blades in general, I suspect you are of a similar sort to Keira, whether Valkyrie or not."

"Yet Keira always fought to defend Ulrik," Åse reminded, not about to be impressed despite Athena's obvious skills. "Where Athena seems capable of defending only herself."

"Maybe," Athena conceded, not riled by the assessment. "Yet I have a feeling that might've changed had Zane gone after Týr...or even you, Åse."

"Me?" Åse chuckled and rolled her eyes. "Why when I do not need defending? When you and I are not even kin?"

"I would guess because Týr loves you, and I love him," Athena said matter-of-factly. "That means my inner dragon considers your life as precious as his."

"Foolish beast," Åse muttered and scowled, yet Týr was surprised to feel something stir inside her. Could she be softening toward Athena? With mere *words*? He found that hard to believe.

"Unless, of course," Athena murmured into his mind, *"Åse isn't as immune to love as she lets the world think."*

"*She does not love me, though.*" His inner voice was gruff with emotion as he admitted how he felt about Athena. What he had come to realize. "*Not the way you and I love each other.*"

"*No, she doesn't love you in that way,*" Athena agreed. "*But perhaps she loves someone else like that? The woman she keeps at the Fortress?*"

"*Hilda?*" he exclaimed. He knew Åse cared a great deal for her, but *love*? It seemed hard to believe. Åse had always been so free with her affections rather than devoted to any one person.

Athena didn't respond, but she didn't need to. Her suggestion gave him much to mull over as they traveled. Namely, that he might have missed something so important despite how close he and Åse were. Worse yet, he'd missed it because he had grown accustomed to what she'd provided him physically. Something she might've continued providing for him because she worried about him when she may have wanted to settle down with Hilda.

"Look," Athena exclaimed softly, pointing ahead. "Do you see them?"

"*Ja.*" He stopped and shaded his eyes against the last rays of sunlight being swallowed up by black windswept clouds. "There are two baby dragons this time..."

He trailed off when intense emotion swept over him at the sight of not just her little blue dragon but a small black one as well. There could be no doubt it was him in another life. It was seeing hers in this place, however, that impacted him so strongly. That made breathing a struggle.

"Just like seeing yours impacts me so strongly," Athena said softly. She pushed up her sleeve and held out her arm, only to reveal a second dragon on her tattoo. Identical to the pattern on his shield, it was back-to-back with the first dragon. She blinked back tears as she looked from where the tiny dragons had been moments before to the tattoo. "You were so important to me...yet I can't remember much more..."

"You will," he assured gently, sure of it as he rubbed his fingers over the tattoo to soothe her skin. Soothe *her*. "We both will. I'm sure of it."

"By following their lead," she murmured, glancing up at the mouth of the cave they'd scurried into, then back to him. "Because they want to show us something. *Remind* us of something." It seemed like a shadow crossed over her face when she looked that way again, and her voice turned breathy with awe. "But so does he."

"Who?" Careful not to step too close and upset Týr's inner beast, Rafe rested his hand on Athena's shoulder and went perfectly still. So still, his attire momentarily flickered to black wizard robes, and he knew his cousin sensed something he couldn't. "Tell me more, Athena. Let me see who tries to lure you into his web."

"Someone who needs me," she whispered, her eyes not quite right. Glazed as she stared at the mountain. "Someone calling to me."

"Do not listen to him," Týr growled, not liking this one bit. He went to pull her into his arms to keep her from being lured by whoever called her, but Rafe shook his head, his eyes shining as white as the snow around them with his magic.

"Do you know him, Athena?" Rafe went on, clearly trying to figure out if it was Zane influencing her somehow. "Have you met him in this life?"

She went to respond, but whatever had gripped her fled, and her eyes cleared, leaving her confused.

"What just happened?" she said shakily, looking around in alarm. "Where did Zane go? When did we travel all this way?" She

160

blinked several times before she seemed to regain her memory. "Never mind...I remember now...I think."

He fought back fear at this unknown entity's strange, random grip over her. How easily he could get inside her mind without Týr sensing him there. Because he was certain he'd been able to navigate around Ulrik and do the same with Keira on their venture.

So, should he give up the quest for his shield now and get Athena far away from all this? Steal her away despite Loki's prophecy, to hell with what happened to dragonkind and even the world? Although more than tempted, he knew she would not go easily, so best to stay the course for now and die protecting her if and when the time came.

"Was it Zane influencing her?" Týr asked Rafe as his cousin pulled his hand away. "Tell me it was Zane, so I at least have a target."

He didn't want to have to kill his cousin, but it would be better than his mate being killed, and that told him just how close they had become. Just how powerful his love for her was.

"I cannot say who he is," Rafe said darkly, clearly uneasy. "Only that he is very good at evading me. So good that I'm inclined to think he's blood-related."

"Which aligns with Keira being lured toward danger before, too," Åse said. "Lured toward danger by someone on the inside. Somebody who is very likely kin."

"Only Keira wasn't exactly lured toward danger, was she?" Athena said. Her gaze returned to the cave entrance above. "In the end, she was lured toward a better outcome than anyone saw coming."

"Even so." Rafe shot Týr a warning glance to keep an eye on her because whatever had been down in that mud volcano with them had meant to end not just them but her specifically. Or so it had seemed. "You cannot trust whoever this is, Athena, if for no other reason than their lack of transparency. If they are kin and evasive about what they know, you must consider them dangerous and not to be trusted."

"Even though I trust you," she replied softly. "When you have kin that find you evasive about what you know."

Although Rafe seemed unaffected by her words, Týr felt how much they wounded him. Felt what his cousin rarely let others feel for one vulnerable moment before Rafe closed off, eyed the sky, and continued climbing, claiming they should get to the cave before the storm arrived because it would be bad.

"I'm sorry," Athena murmured into Týr's mind as he helped her up a slick incline. *"He didn't deserve that. Especially given he came to my defense earlier. It seems my dragon's speaking before my human half can stop it, and she's obviously not the nicest."*

"I think it has more to do with whoever this is influencing you than your inner beast having an impulsive tongue," he replied. *"Fear not, mate. Rafe has long hardened his heart to words others might find disagreeable."*

"Nevertheless, he deserved better than that from me." She sighed, squinting against the increasingly gusty wind. *"Honestly, I had been hopeful that just maybe..."*

"He and Quinn would be a match?" he guessed, following her thoughts when she trailed off. *"That she would cheer him up some?"*

"She does have a way about her," Athena said. *"But he seems so set against it...her."* She hesitated before continuing. *"So why did he take a vow of celibacy, if you don't mind me asking? Is he some sort of wizardly priest?"*

"I cannot say what he's considered with the Celts," he said. *"Nor can I say why he's denied himself pleasures of the flesh other than he's*

strongly committed to it. I get the sense he feels breaking this vow will have dire consequences. Ones he's long kept shrouded from his kin."

"Even from Mea?"

"That I cannot answer other than to say she would be the only one to know if, in fact, he has shared."

"It is too bad the entrance is not further up," Åse commented, drawing them out of their private conversation. She grinned up at the sheer rock face above the cave entrance. "That would have been fun to climb."

"On that, we agree." Athena gazed up at it as well. "Tricky but definitely fun." When Åse looked at her in surprise, his mate shrugged. "What? I might not be in the best shape, but I still love a good challenge. Especially if I get to discover new things along the way."

"You are not in that bad of shape," Åse said under her breath as they continued toward the entrance. "Now that you are embracing your inner beast, you should see improvement where it's needed."

Týr bit back a grin at the hint of a truce between the women. Moreover, whether she'd admit it or not, Åse was of the same mind as him. Athena's shape was perfect, just as it was. Something seen moments later when the last thing they saw coming crashed into them.

-Her Viking Dragon Warrior-

Chapter Seventeen

"NO," ATHENA ROARED when a deep, terrifying rumble resounded, and the ground shook seconds before an avalanche crashed over the cave entrance. She didn't think, only saw red and acted, putting her back to it and bracing her legs, determined to protect Týr, Åse, and Rafe.

Using more magic than she knew she possessed, she held it back for what seemed several searingly painful minutes but was likely only seconds before Rafe pushed past the magic behind the blasting snow and chanted them into the cave out of harm's way. For a moment, she thought she was okay, but realized a blink later she was no such thing. When her knees buckled, Týr scooped her up before she hit the floor and pursued Rafe when he urged them to follow him.

"We need to get away from whatever that was," Rafe said. "It possesses the same magic I felt in the storm that kept Ulrik from going after Keira on their journey, then again at the mud volcano.

The same magic that belongs to whoever betrayed us from the inside."

Athena tried to reply either aloud or telepathically but felt ridiculously drained. Embarrassingly so.

"You should not feel such, though," Týr said into her mind. *"What you did back there was truly courageous, just as Rafe said you would be. Too courageous for my taste."*

That said something, considering how much he valued bravery. His heart hammered in her ear as he followed Rafe, and Åse took up the rear with her weapon drawn. She felt his awe and respect but also his anger at her willingness to put herself in harm's way for him. For any of them.

She wasn't sure where they were going, but it seemed Týr did, claiming their young dragons from another life led the way. He directed Rafe until they ended up in a small cave system higher up that was close enough to an entrance to provide fresh air yet back far enough to keep firelight from prying eyes.

"How do you feel, Athena?" Týr rumbled softly, sitting on a rock in front of a fire Åse chanted to life while Rafe saw to food and drink. Staples, it seemed, with these Viking dragons. Týr stroked her hair and waited, the tension in his strong body palpable.

"I'm okay," she whispered, grateful to find her voice worked, but barely she was so parched.

"Here." Rafe crouched in front of them and held a cup of cold water to her mouth. "Drink, *brennende en.*"

Athena tried, but the moment she went to sip, she ended up coughing instead. Then, she coughed even more when dragging in air became impossible, and she began choking.

The more she choked, the more the world darkened.

166

"She suffers from the same thing I did after the mud volcano," Åse said from what seemed a great distance away before Athena found herself on her knees, braced up by the Viking woman who was also on her knees. Yet it seemed to do the trick because, at last, she was finally able to drag in air.

As Åse held her, she continued coughing from so much smoke it was a wonder she was still alive. Finally, at last, the coughing subsided, and she was able to gulp in life-giving oxygen again. She wasn't sure how long she clung onto Åse, only that she was once more embarrassed when she finally found the strength to let go.

"You need not be embarrassed," Åse said gruffly. She gripped Athena's shoulder to make sure she was stable, wrapped her hand around the back of Athena's neck, and looked at her in a whole new way. One she didn't expect. "You are no longer *svak en*, weak one, but *sterk en*, strong one." She clenched her jaw, squelching emotions as quickly as she felt them, by the looks of it. "And you are no longer my enemy but my sister."

What to say to that? She had no clue other than it felt right. Overdue. And she wasn't entirely sure why because it wasn't for obvious reasons but part of all this somehow.

Åse was part of her somehow.

Yet there was no way to voice that, so she nodded and blinked back unexpected tears. "I like the sound of that, Åse." She managed a weak smile and glanced from Týr, who hovered nearby, clearly worried about her, back to his friend. "I imagine it will make life easier for Týr going forward."

A slow smile curled Åse's mouth in return. "I imagine so." She narrowed her eyes, challenging Athena. "Are you ready to stand, *sterk en?*"

"I am," she confirmed, feeling stronger by the moment.

"Good." Åse stood and held out her hand. "Then stand, sister."

Rather than hesitate and let Åse see even an ounce of weakness, she clasped her hand and stood, relieved when her legs felt strong. When *she* felt strong.

Åse squeezed her hand and nodded once in approval before stepping away. When Týr stepped forward to grab her if she went down, she shook her head and stayed him with her hand.

"I'm okay." She looked at him with confidence she knew he needed to see. "I really am." She rubbed her dry lips together. "Albeit, thirsty."

"Then drink, friend." Rafe handed her the cup of water he'd tried to hold to her mouth before. "As much as you can to fight off dehydration."

She couldn't help but smile at how modern he sounded as she took the cup and drank, thanking him with a grateful look when he handed her a second after she chugged down the first. What was with all the deadly smoke? How did it all tie together, because she was certain it did, whether it had to do with their unseen enemy or not.

"I'm sorry, Rafe," she said softly after finishing the second cup. She still felt bad about reminding him he was as elusive as their enemy. "I shouldn't have said what I did earlier."

"No need for apologies." He gestured she sit in one of several chairs he'd manifested around the fire. "Whether influenced by our enemy or merely your dragon looking out for its mate, you were right. I do have kin who find me evasive about what I know. Plenty of them, for that matter."

"Even so, I shouldn't have said it like that, so I am sorry if for no other reason than I believe you keep secrets to protect your kin rather than the other way around." She thought about what he'd said earlier because she truly did have a great deal of respect for him, either because she related with him being ostracized most of his life or because her dragon simply trusted him. "Is the avalanche what you were talking about when you said it was only a matter of time before everyone saw how courageous I am?" She shook her head, unconvinced. "Because, to be honest, I'm not entirely sure *what* I did."

"Yes, you are." Rafe gazed at her much like Åse had moments before. "You did whatever it took to protect your mate from harm as well as those he cares about. Those you knew would protect him if anything happened to you." He considered her for a moment. "At least that was your initial reaction before you and your dragon protected us because we did not deserve death." He seemed to want to say one thing but said another instead with an unmistakable glint of admiration in his eyes. "As to what I said on the ship, no. What you did back there was the least of how courageous you can truly be, *sterk en*."

Before she could reply, he stood and gestured at Åse to join him. "Fighting that avalanche made you expel far more magic than you're used to, Athena, so you need rest. Åse and I will scout these caves and keep watch over things while the storm rages, then we will continue on in the morn when it lets up."

"Shouldn't we keep moving now?" she argued, but her words fell on deaf ears because Rafe and Åse were already gone.

"He's right." Clearly done with allowing her to stand strong on her own two feet, Týr scooped her up and sat in front of the fire with her on his lap. "You might feel strong at the moment, but I suspect that has more to do with finally measuring up to a forgiving Åse than anything else." The corner of his mouth twitched in amusement. "Or should I say, having your moment of triumph over her because she finally saw what I've seen all along."

"You did not," she chastised. "In fact, I'm relatively certain you thought I was equally weak when we first met."

"Weak?" His eyebrows shot up, and he teased. "If anything, I thought you a worthy opponent because you were able to steal my weapons several times over."

"Not knowingly," she argued but met his small smile. "And while I'm not proud of what has to be my inner beast's actions, I'll admit I'm grateful to her."

"Me, too," he murmured, at last letting down his guard enough that she felt how intensely he'd feared for her earlier. His deep-rooted horror when she'd taken the brunt of hundreds of tons of ice-packed snow traveling at over eighty miles per hour to save him and his kin.

"Don't ever do that again, *brennende liten kompis,*" he said softly, cupping her cheek as if she were the most precious thing in the world. His gaze roamed her face before he looked her in the eyes, meaning every word. "Do not put my life above yours."

She could respond with all sorts of endearments she would have been incapable of saying, let alone feeling, days ago but knew only one thing would make sense to him. "What would you say if I asked the same of you?"

He inhaled deeply, understanding, and answered the only way he could. "That I could never promise you that." He shook his head. "Would not promise it because I would be incapable."

"Exactly." She rested her hand on his chest. "Then we understand each other." And because she was emboldened by Rafe and Åse's faith in courage she'd had no idea she possessed. "From one warrior to another, we understand each other."

Despite his inner dragon's flail of defiance seen clearly in the fiery burn of his eyes, Týr rested his hand over hers and conceded. "It seems we might."

"Good."

170

"Good." Concern flared in his eyes. "That said, you need to eat and regain your strength. You need to—"

"I *do* need to," she conceded softly yet stayed his hand when he reached for a piece of meat off the platter Rafe had manifested. "But not with food...not yet."

"Food is the only way to—"

Before he could finish his sentence, she cupped his cheeks and closed her mouth over his. Kissed him with a sense of gratefulness at first for surviving the day, then with an overwhelming need that roared up with such vivid intensity she lost her breath all over again.

She did not, however, lose her courage as she broke the kiss long enough to straddle him. Nor did she lose her newfound bravery as she met his eyes and slowly undid the strings on her tunic until she could pull the garment over her head and toss it aside.

Relishing curves men in her past might have found less than appealing, he feasted his eyes on her full breasts in a way that made her feel sinfully voluptuous. Every bit as beautiful and desirable as her friends.

"Because you are," he rumbled, fondling first one breast then another before he pulled an overly sensitive nipple into his mouth and suckled hard enough to send a jolt of searing heat through her.

Driven by the delicious sensations fanning out from her core, she ground her hips against his rigid length, eager to feel him deep inside her again. Desperate for it.

So desperate, in fact, she chanted them free of their clothing without realizing it and sank onto him, only to shutter and whimper when a full-blown climax rippled through her. Clearly practiced at bringing women pleasure, he squeezed her backside with one strong hand and pressed his hips up so he went deeper still, hitting all sorts of nerve endings while trailing his fingers lightly up her spine. As he knew it would, the delicious combination of the two sensations made her climax keep going and going.

"Týr," she groaned against his neck, a prisoner to how he made her feel. A slave to pleasure when he eventually squeezed both butt cheeks and steered her slowly up and down his broad shaft. So slowly, invoking so much raw, primal pleasure, she kept whimpering, almost mewling, as intense orgasmic waves continued washing over her.

"More," she gasped, rubbing her cheek against his scratchy beard like a good little dragon against her master. "I want to feel...all of you..."

He clearly caught her thoughts and understood because he grunted with approval and moved faster. So fast that she squirmed in delight and let him have his way until he wrapped her up in his arms, buried a roar in her hair, and let go. When he throbbed deep inside her, and his liquid heat filled her pulsing flesh, she sailed right off a cliff of sheer ecstasy.

They stayed that way for a while, struggling to catch their breath. Basked in pleasure. Relished one another's heat. Eventually, he steered her mouth back to his and kissed her so passionately there could be no doubt how much he cared for her. Kissed her so deeply, stirring their passion again, that she doubted there would be any eating tonight.

"But there will be," he murmured against her lips before he pulled back and had her sitting on his lap wrapped in a fur in one swift movement. "Because you need to eat and regain your strength, *brennende liten kompis.* I will not have you weakened and vulnerable against whatever lies ahead."

When she pouted, wanting to get back to lovemaking, he smirked. "It seems you really are as insatiable as me."

"So it seems." But would that be enough? She frowned the more she thought about it. About all of this. Him. Her. The future she would leave behind if she stayed with him.

Following her thoughts, he tensed and met her frown as he fed her a piece of succulent meat. "Yet you will stay with me, *ja*?" His eyebrows edged together. "You will stay with your mate after we retrieve my shield?"

"I don't know." Honestly, she hadn't given it much thought. *Could* she live in this era? In a medieval period lacking so much scientific advancement? While that in itself was certainly daunting, interestingly enough, it wasn't her biggest concern. "What if I *did* stay?" She swallowed back unexpected emotion the more she thought about it. "You're clearly not the monogamous type, and I am." She shook her head. "I can't see you being satisfied with one woman the rest of your life, and I can't imagine anything worse than sharing you with others."

"It seems you do not fully feel my inner beast yet if you question what I'm capable of when it comes to you, mate." He wiped a bit of juice from the corner of her mouth with the pad of his thumb, then licked the liquid in a way that made clear he imagined it coming from another area altogether. "Had you said such days ago, I might have agreed, but no more. Now I am a slave to pleasuring you and you alone for as long as you'll have me." Seductive fire flared in his eyes. "And if ever the day comes you turn me away, I will keep my distance but end any male you take afterward. Any male who dares touch you."

Telling heat blossomed between her thighs at how serious he was. How ruthless his intent could be when it came to her. While she would have thought his line of thinking barbaric and terrifying before, now she reveled in his admission. His pure possessiveness.

"And what if you do get bored with me? What if—"

He put a finger to her lips and shook his head once, making things clear. "I will never, *brennende liten kompis*, for it would be a waste of time. I now know no other can give me such pleasure, and that will never change. It's a certainty buried deep inside my dragon. An instinct that will always keep me faithful."

"I believe you," she murmured, feeling his truth as if it were her own. Understanding him on a level she'd never understood another. This meant he understood her in return and would do everything he could to keep her here. They would talk about it. Have to. But not right now. Instead, she wanted to keep getting to know this side of him better.

The man rather than the beast.

"What happened here?" she said softly, tracing her finger gently along the scar that cut down his face. It suited him somehow. Added to his rough, masculine handsomeness. "I felt the battles behind your other scars, but not this one."

"Zane," he muttered, feeding her another piece of meat. "When we were boys."

"And here I thought you'd have some great war story." She frowned and tried not to shiver at the mention of his cousin. While he was admittedly attractive in a vicious sort of way with his tats and piercings, there was something particularly unnerving about him. Something simmered beneath the surface she didn't trust.

"It *is* a great war story, though," Týr countered, referring to how he'd gotten his scar. He grinned with obvious pride. "I wanted to be the greatest warrior, and I was, *am*, even above Ulrik if he doesn't use his magic." He shrugged. "Zane was the last of my brethren to challenge me after I beat the others in fair one-on-one battles to achieve my status."

"Good God, did he need to be so brutal?"

"Always." Týr looked at her as if she had two heads. "A true warrior never holds back but fights with everything in him. Fights with his head, heart, and blade until the bitter end."

"Yet here you are both still alive," she pointed out.

He winked. "Only because I allowed it." A twinkle lit his eyes as he reflected fondly on the memory. "It was one of the best moments I ever shared with Zane. A bonding of sorts despite his wounded ego. A dragon healer could have taken care of my facial wound, but I refused it. I earned it, and so I wear it with pride."

"You should because it looks good on you." She pressed her lips against the jagged flesh, then met his eyes and issued a small smile. "I'm sure it couldn't hurt to remind Zane of that day going forward. Not just of your victory but of your bond so he never forgets it. Remembers it during the times when his darker personality takes over."

"*Ja*, you know me well already, mate." Only distracted for so long, he fed her another piece of meat. "And you will know me better still if that is what you wish. Both sides of me so well the thought of leaving me will become impossible."

It turned out his arrogance was well-founded because after talking for hours, the idea of leaving him *did* seem more and more impossible. Then again, the more she got to know him, the more his memories became hers and hers, his. She understood it wasn't just their human halves bonding but their inner beasts. Or should she say, rediscovering each other because it felt more like that.

"What about Rune?" she wondered. "I know all of you were closer to her at one time, friends all, so what happened? Why do I sense this great divide now? Is it because of her love affair with the enemy? With Jørn?"

"Not really, as their love is pure speculation." He thought about it. "While I cared for Rune, I always found her pushy when we were children. Always needing to be in control of everything and it seems that hasn't changed much. At some point, Rafe would be the better one to ask about her as they were far closer." He shrugged, clearly having a one-track mind when it came to Rune. "Nowadays, Rune is more evasive than ever and clearly knows more than she's willing to admit, so I, as I do in all things, stand by Ulrik in keeping her at arm's length."

"Yet you trust my friends are safe with her?" Athena asked, even though she already knew the answer.

"While initially, I would have said no, with you and Keira safely in your mate's care now, thanks to her, I'm more inclined to think she stands on the right side of our warring kingdoms."

"Me too," she murmured. "Very much so."

She had more questions about what had divided him and his cousins but sensed it was not a conversation he wanted to have right now. Whatever had happened, because she sensed it began even before Zane and Knud's falling out, it tore apart not only a family but eight good childhood friends. Ulrik, Týr, Rafe, Zane, Magnus, Åse, Mea and Rune. Which made her wonder where Jørn fit in. Either way, they had been a sizeable group of dear friends at one time, so it was sad such division existed now.

They continued talking about random everyday things, but she sensed Týr tiring of their conversation when he began dropping random kisses. Peppered them here and there until he took the words out of her mouth entirely and reminded her of the other reason she would be helpless against fleeing him.

A reason that would shake them both to their core and end up surprising him every bit as much as it did her.

-Her Viking Dragon Warrior-

Chapter Eighteen

FROM THE MOMENT Týr sensed Athena might leave him and return to the future, he was determined to change her mind. Through words, kisses, or gentle caresses, he would wage a battle to keep her by his side with everything in him. Show her how bonded they already were. Let her in like he had no other and make her see what he knew to be true.

They *were* fated mates, so they could only ever find their way back to each other.

He couldn't leave his people; they had to be protected, so she had to come to him. Stay here always as his mate. His queen. The only dragon he would have in his bed until someday they dined in the great halls of Valhalla together.

So he had to find a way. Figure it out. Somehow give her the future and the present both. Give her it all if she would only let him because everything about her beguiled him, from their endless conversations to the way her lips felt beneath his. The softness of her thighs around his waist. The warmth of her tight sheath gripping his cock.

Something he eventually grew impatient for again in a whole new way. Because the more she opened up to him and her sensuality flowered, the more he wanted to show her what it could really be like between dragons. The rough bed sport inherent to their kind and the immense pleasure that came with it.

Granted, he had found far more pleasure than he'd expected in what they'd already shared, but he wanted to take her one step further. Own her flesh in a way she would never be able to get enough of. Brand her soft, vulnerable curves with sinful, addictive memories she would want to reenact often. Several times a day, at the very least.

That in mind, he set to seducing her throughout their conversation until she gave in to a deep, tongue-tangling kiss she couldn't escape until he was good and ready. Which wasn't until the scent of her arousal became too much to bear, giving him no choice but to chant them out of their clothes so he could lay her on furs beside the fire. Close enough to feed both her addictions.

Him and the flames.

While there were a thousand different ways he could go about this, one craving rose above the others, so he flipped her on her belly. Although his arousal throbbed painfully at the sight of her lush backside, he brushed aside her silky hair and took his time. He nipped and kissed and bit his way from the back of her sensitive neck to her shoulder blades to the flare of her waist until he nipped one well-rounded buttock hard enough to make her yelp.

When she squirmed, and the scent of her arousal became that much stronger, he grinned and nipped the other cheek, then yanked her back onto her knees. He stilled when he realized just how rough he'd been. Had it been too much? Should he slow down? He swore his heart stopped thinking she didn't like it. Wouldn't want it.

Instead, much to his relief, she ramped up his arousal even more when she seemed to understand exactly what he wanted. Expected of her. Or, based on the rampant lust he felt swirling in her mind, wanted the same because she sank her breasts onto the furs, widened her knees, and arched her back, offering herself up like the good little dragon she'd thought herself earlier.

Pleased, he grabbed her hips and licked his lips at the sight of her. A view that pulled his inner Helheim to the surface in a way that had never happened before. A way that alarmed him initially until he realized she was responding to it.

Better yet, she had invoked it.

Either way, when she rested her cheek on the fur and her inner dragon flamed in her eyes with a deep, drenching lust, both sides of him came together in perfect synchronicity. Even better, he knew with absolute certainty she could handle both sides. Craved them.

And it made him see dragonly red in all its wonderful, beastly brilliance.

After that, any hope of holding back was stripped away, and he penetrated her in one long, unforgiving thrust. She cried out and dug her fists into the fur before shuddering and groaning with approval.

He could hardly breathe with the sheer pleasure of it. With the sight of his thickness stretching her tender, gripping flesh. If he had the self-restraint to keep admiring how stunning she looked submitting to him, he would, but his body needed hers like a dragon needed wings to fly.

So he took her with a new ferociousness born of everything in him, from his Midgard side to his wicked inner Helheim. Slammed into her again and again with long, deep, jarring strokes fueled by her groans, moans, and throaty dragonly purrs. Took her as he dug his hand into her hair, wrapped an arm around her waist, and pulled her back against him.

Then he took her some more while rubbing the apex at the center of her pleasure until she was sobbing and soaked. Her slick skin sheened blue with her inner dragon as she jerked against him and released so hard, clamping down on him tightly, that she forced him to her will, and he roared with the pleasure of spilling his seed deep inside her once again.

In fact, he roared so loudly, and his blood pounded so thickly through his veins, it took him several long moments to realize her tears of pleasure had turned to tears of sadness. He tilted her chin until she was forced to look over her shoulder at him. "What is it?"

Because oddly, he couldn't sense it in her mind.

"This," she whispered hoarsely, pointing at her tattoo. "Look...do you see it? *Feel* it?"

A circle with runic symbols had formed between the back-to-back dragons, mimicking the design on his shield once again. One he had looked at hundreds of times over the years but never thought about until now.

"*Why?*" he ground out, feeling the division the circle represented with such acute pain and such an intense sense of rejection he understood instantly what it meant. "You shunned me in our last life." He could hardly believe it as he gazed into her eyes. "I don't understand...why would you shun me?"

"I don't know." She swallowed hard, closed her eyes as if struggling to find the answer, then looked back at him again. "Maybe it has something to do with my nightmare."

"What nightmare?" He frowned and repositioned them until she was on his lap again. "Tell me."

So she did, explaining how she'd raced toward an eruption determined to save the people in the village below, only for a masculine voice to try and stop her.

"It was you," she said softly, still sadly eyeing her tattoo. "I'm certain of it."

"Was I a dragon? Were you?"

"Yes." She nodded, then shook her head. "At least I was. I'm not sure about you."

"Yet we were mates," he reminded, never surer of anything. When he finally touched the tattoo, he felt such intense emotional pain he flinched. "So says this tattoo. So says my shield."

"Or so we imagine." Athena's worried gaze met his. "What if we were like Ulrik and Keira? Longing for love but divided because we were two different creatures?"

"No." He shook his head slowly. "That doesn't feel right. We were here together before just as we are now...just as..."

"Dragons," she murmured, picking up on the same feeling. "Not shifters but full-blooded dragons."

"Yet divided somehow in the end." He clenched his teeth and fought a wave of fear mixed with rage because, again, he was certain he was right. "You shunned me somehow. Ended what we had found together."

Athena released a shaky sigh, and her eyes welled anew. "Yes." She shook her head. "I feel like I should remember why, but it's just out of reach. Impossible to latch on to." She cupped his cheek and looked at him with her heart in her eyes. "I'm so sorry, though. Whatever happened back then, I'm so terribly sorry because it feels like..." She seemed to struggle to find the right words as a tear slipped down her cheek. "It feels like I had to have caused us both a great deal of pain."

He might be angry and hurt over their mysterious past-life separation, but her sorrow was his, and he wouldn't allow it. So he wrapped her up in his arms and soothed her the best he could. Conflicting emotions or not, he was incapable of anything else. Both his human and dragon cherished her too much.

"Whatever happened in our last life, it is not this one, Athena," he finally said after she muddled through the same tidal wave of emotions as him. He tilted her chin until her bloodshot eyes met his and wiped away her tears. "This time, we are warriors both and will fight with everything in us to keep history from repeating itself."

While he, in part, implied his hope that she never leave him, he also meant it literally. He had seen what she was capable of by holding back that avalanche, so he knew a great and courageous warrior lived within her. He'd seen hints of it in her ability to confiscate and wield other people's blades in the blink of an eye.

When she didn't reply right away, he brushed his lips across hers and spoke tender words he never thought he'd utter to a woman. "I will fight for you always, *brennende liten kompis,* because I love you. *In* love for the first time in this life when I thought such impossible."

"I love you too," she whispered, her voice raspy with emotion. "I don't know how I know when I've never been in love, but I do. I am." She pressed her lips together and nodded as another tear slipped free. "With you...very much so."

He had heard from his parents, aunts, uncles, and elders how jarring it could be to find love with someone you'd known mere days, especially if you had never experienced the emotion before, but this felt anything but jarring. Rather, it felt like a piece of him had been missing for far too long. A crucial piece that made everything seem far more vivid and bright. Better somehow despite the turbulent times in which he lived and their precarious situation at the moment.

A situation he wanted to rectify with more comforting kisses as he wiped away her tears again. More caresses if only to soothe her. Yet he knew they might never stop if he did, and she needed to rest.

"You need sleep, mate," he murmured, fighting the urge to kiss her. "More than you realize if you hope to regain your strength."

So he laid her on the fur and pulled her back against his front before covering them. Then, with all the power he could muster, he tried to will away an erection that seemed unending.

"Týr," she pleaded so softly he barely caught it, but he understood what she needed, so he slipped into her from behind and kept with small, even movements. Just enough to keep them at a lower simmer of pleasure. Or so he'd hoped until she made that purring sound unique to her dragon that drove his inner beast to distraction.

He would make many offspring with her if only to hear that sound always. As often as possible. As often as it took to...not just hear that sound but give her children. Give *them* children.

She seemed as startled and aroused by his thoughts as he based on the way she stilled and steered his hand to her belly. Her response wasn't one of thought but more primal. Evocative. As though her inner beast wanted him to warm her womb from the inside out. As if it relished the idea of children every bit as much as him.

Even though they should probably talk about this, discuss where she stood when her mind wasn't clouded with desire and lust, he couldn't manage a word if he tried. Could not stop from drowning in a whole new type of pleasure as he moved within her. As an instinct as old as time took over.

A need he never thought he'd crave made everything fade away, but the feel of her in his arms. All around him. Welcoming him when he ground deep, his ballocks tightened, and he let go deep inside her. In response, she shuddered and bore down on him, her sheath welcoming all he had to offer.

He remained locked inside her afterward, never more content as everything became a blur of deep relaxation. At least until he dozed off because the next thing he knew, he was caught in a dream, racing up a wooded smoke-filled mountain, not just in dragon form but in a sheer state of panic.

"Duck!" he roared at a shimmering blue female dragon as chunks of molten rock crashed down all around her. Fear rocketed through him when he realized it was Athena in what had to be a different life. He bolted after her, dodging left and right as fiery projectiles slammed to the ground and ash rained down in an ever-thickening white-out.

"I should have known," she gasped. "I thought I did."

Known what? About what was happening? About what was clearly a massive volcanic eruption?

"No," she roared, turning back in anger. Confrontation. "I can't be wrong!"

She said nothing more, but he heard her thoughts when her pained eyes met his. How she felt it was her duty to protect him and so many others. When her eyes drifted over his shoulder in alarm, he turned, shocked by what he saw behind him.

Stunned because he suddenly understood with heartbreaking clarity what she intended to do. Shocked because he sensed something he knew even she didn't yet, because her gift, who she was, would always protect him first and foremost, even if it meant hiding the truth from her dragon.

She had to know, though.

He had to stop her.

Yet when he turned back, she had already fled and didn't hear his roars of denial. Did not hear his heartbreak when she raced into certain death and forfeited so much more than she ever could have imagined.

Chapter Nineteen

"**W**AKE UP, ATHENA!" Quinn roared into her mind. *"Wake up now before he finds it!"*

Athena bolted upright, confused, trying to figure out where Quinn was. What was she talking about? But she wasn't there. Instead, Týr was sound asleep beside her, and their baby dragons stared at her from a break in the cave wall that led outside.

Her little dragon leapt from foot to foot and looked at her expectantly before she blew a tiny stream of fire at his dragon as if warning him to stay away and whipped out of the cave. Týr's little dragon roared in denial, looked at Athena with pure, unfiltered terror that was solely for her tiny dragon's safety, and raced after her.

Just as fearful because she knew something terrible was going to happen, she chanted into her clothes and raced after them. She skidded to a halt at the edge of what seemed a sky-high drop, only to find them struggling mid-flight in a snow-driven wind shear that would slam them into the ground far below.

It didn't matter if they were likely manifestations of their previous incarnations. She could not, *would* not, let harm come to Týr, so she shifted and leapt after them, only for everything to fall away and her environment to warp entirely.

Just like her nightmare, she once again raced up an erupting volcano and knew she dreamt, except this time, it seemed so much more vivid. More real as she dodged fiery projectiles that crashed down around her.

Everything became painfully clear when a masculine roar pleaded for her to turn back. Especially when her eyes locked on the male dragon behind her, and she saw Týr so clearly within him. Saw the deep love and connection they shared.

Saw how she had vowed to protect him always.

Would die a thousand times over to keep him safe.

Then she looked over his shoulder and saw so much more. First, a young woman raced after them with tears in her eyes before she fell to her knees, choking on the cloying smoke. One so familiar, Athena nearly lost her footing.

Åse? Could it be? Yet she knew it was.

She had no time to process that because what loomed behind Åse caught her attention. A village nestled below at the foot of a much different Beerenberg on the northern side of the isle. A silent, proud mountain full of not ice and snow but trees and greenery. A habitable mountain that nourished the community at its feet.

So what mountain had she been racing up?

It felt like the life drained out of her as she turned and looked up at the behemoth mountain behind her, puffing ash and smoke at the sky.

"Good *God*," she whispered, caught somewhere between reality and what she experienced. Terror. Awe. A dream? A memory? "There was once a *supervolcano* on the southern part of this isle?"

She had no time to wrap her mind around that before she was caught in what had to be a dream and raced up the mountain once again in dragon form. Raced to stop an astronomical amount of death and destruction. More than anyone could possibly imagine because this beast made Yellowstone look like an undergrown fire ant trying to measure up to a hundred full-grown male dragons roaring their mightiest fire simultaneously.

While there was proof of a much smaller though extinct volcano here, how was there no archaeological record of this being a supervolcano? Some proof of its existence? It made no sense. No evidence of a volcano this monstrous was scientifically impossible.

Yet science seemed irrelevant to her dragon as she kept racing upward, determined, it seemed, to stop the beast somehow. She had but one motive. Save Týr and the village below. Better still, Åse. His *person*. Because outside of Athena, she had meant everything to him.

She set aside her heartache from leaving him and crashed through the trees because taking flight in this ash would be as lethal to her wings as ash in an engine. The sheer weight would drop her. Hinder her ability to fly every bit as much as it would a commercial airliner trying to pass over.

"I will not let you go, mate," Týr roared from somewhere behind her. Close behind her, at that. Too close, yet when he roared more words, she couldn't quite catch them.

His proximity made her push harder because she knew, without question, he would leap into the volcano instead and use every bit of dragon magic he had to stop it. He would forfeit his life for her and for the world as he knew it. Caught in this strange waking reality, Athena realized this was the moment Loki had been talking about. *This* was Týr's certain death, not in their current life but in their past one.

Either way, she refused to let it happen.

If she were able to get to a certain point, he wouldn't be able to go any further. She knew it without question but wasn't sure why. Afterward, she could only pray to Odin that she could fix this. That she could make things right because this was happening far sooner than she thought it would.

There had been no time to evacuate.

No time to save so many.

Or so she'd thought back then, where her modern self knew if a volcano this immense fully erupted, it would likely kill off most human and animal life within a year or two.

All that aside, the eruption was coming too soon, and she felt the powerful magic connected to it. The same magic she'd felt in the mud volcano. The same magic present in the flames that had taken Keira's Valkyrie dragon in her previous life.

"*No,*" she roared into Týr's mind, terrified he might catch up with her too soon. That he would forfeit his life for her and, in turn, risk everything. So she said all she could. What would wound him most. "*I shun you, mate. I do not want you anymore!*"

Just as her tattoo had insinuated.

And it broke her heart every bit as much as she knew it did his because dragon mates shunning one another was a million times worse than breaking up with a boyfriend or girlfriend. A trillion times worse than divorce.

She felt his pain every bit as much as her own, but she had no choice. None at all as she raced upward and gathered more power than she ever imagined possible. Power that made her vision haze red, then gold, as she manifested an invisible wall that kept him from going any further. Meanwhile, having no choice but to fly this last leg as lava rolled like a living, writhing, fiery beast down the mountainside, she leapt into the smoke-ridden air.

After that, her world dwindled down to the monster she hoped to conquer, and it was a mighty demon as it began to explode. An unfathomably vicious beast she would never be able to tame, but she had to try.

Would die trying if that's what it took.

And it would, she realized with absolute certainty, finally remembering what her dragon had decided to do. What it *could* do because she was every bit as much a Valkyrie as Keira. This feat, however, was far different than the flames her friend had faced. Far more immense.

Nonetheless, she had to try, so whispering a final goodbye into Týr's mind, she shot down into the flaming crater of deadly gasses. Willed every ounce of her godliness into a shield of sorts and pushed with everything in her. Pushed with all the love she felt for Týr while willing destruction of the beast swallowing her up.

Down, down, down she flew deeper into a vortex of blinding pain and searing heat. So deep, she realized the only way to destroy the volcano was to crash it inward and displace it. A monumental feat she poured every last bit of godly magic she possessed into, opening up tunnels deep beneath the bottom of the sea to release pressure in the lava pockets. Magma chambers and fissures she threaded out to an all-too-familiar location, creating a second volcano deep under the ocean. A location that would someday be known as the Haakon Mosby mud volcano.

The very volcano that had nearly taken their lives the day before.

Even with such an incredible amount of force removed from the erupting volcano, it wasn't enough. Not nearly. So, choking on smoke, she redirected all her energy, the very last of her divine power, into squelching the monster, only to feel so much more power expand from her than expected.

Power that absolutely broke her heart because it was too late to stop it.

She and the child she didn't realize she carried had unleashed a power so immense, so determined to protect her mate and her little one's father, that nothing could stop it once it welled.

Not even the mightiest of supervolcanoes.

"No," she roared in denial moments before the mountain imploded and came crashing down on them in a flash of indescribable blinding pain.

Absolute torture, both inside and out.

Seconds expanded and retracted before everything morphed around her once more, the pain faded, and Zane, of all people, stared down at her in alarm from the snow-swept rocky landscape of what was once the largest volcano the world had ever seen.

Just like that, she was fully awake and free of the past.

Beyond nightmares of certain death and back in the present.

"You must be quiet, woman," he hissed, clamping a hand over her mouth. *"Now."*

Only then did she realize she'd been wailing in grief, and not just snow surrounded her but a bed of simmering embers and ashes. She didn't need modern-day technology to tell her they matched the unusual ashes on the hearth back in Maine. If that wasn't telling enough, she held Týr's smoldering shield against her chest.

A shield that had been born of the magic she and her child had created to save Týr and likely the world. And the dragons on it weren't her and Týr but her and their unborn daughter.

194

"Stop," Zane ground out when she continued sobbing despite his obtrusive hand. He scanned the sky. "You draw them closer, so you *must* stop, Athena."

Yet it seemed it was too late for that when all hell broke loose moments later, and too many dragons to count emerged out of the driving snow and crashed down around them.

She tried to shift to defend herself but was far too drained by what had just happened. It seemed Zane sensed it, too, because the next thing she knew, his giant red dragon towered over her, defending her against several male dragons before he scooped her up and launched into the air.

"Put her down, cousin!" Týr roared into their minds, his fear for her palpable, but it was too late. Zane had dodged incoming dragons intercepted by his commanders and swooped out over the open sea with her and the shield in hand.

Is this what Quinn had meant when she'd startled her awake earlier and said don't let him get it? Had she known all of this would happen to Athena and lead her and the shield right into Zane's waiting talons?

"If I put her down, they'll take her, Týr." Zane ignored Åse and Rafe's equally threatening voices. *"Help fend off these enemy dragons, and I'll get her to the Keep safely. You have my word."*

"I'm okay," she said shakily into Týr's mind, still trying to cope with her overwhelming grief. Even so, she couldn't have her mate so focused on her he wasn't aware of the immense danger around him. *"Zane saved me back there. I don't think he means me any harm."*

"At least not yet," Týr growled, his inner beast in a frenzy at her current position. Her sheer vulnerability.

"Bring her to the Lair," Týr said to Zane. *"My people will keep her safe."*

"Against this many enemy dragons?" Zane replied in amusement. *"I think we both know that isn't true. She will be safer surrounded by my dragons."*

She felt Týr's rage, yet he had no choice but to do as Zane requested and fight off dragons who tried to attack his cousin from every angle. It was alarming they considered her the greater prize, considering what Týr had done to one of their own the day before.

"Nonetheless, you are by far the greater prize, mate," Týr said, his internal voice going in and out as he fought. *"And now you know why."*

She wasn't so sure about that, given she felt so drained. Too drained to possess the power of a Valkyrie. Too heartbroken to be much of a defender of anything or anyone, period. Honestly, Zane could crush her here and now in his mighty grip, and she doubted she'd put up much of a fight. She just didn't have it in her.

"I could not crush you even if I wanted to," Zane rumbled, following her thoughts a little too closely. *"And you will realize that soon enough, sterk en."*

Strong one? Really? Coming from him, of all dragons? She felt anything but, so she was surprised he'd honored her with those words because she didn't need to know him all that well to know dragons like him didn't grant such praise to just anyone.

Every time an enemy dragon swooped too close to Zane, one of his commanders or Týr, Åse, or Rafe were there fending them off until a line of monstrous dragons appeared on the horizon, flying at them like a wall of thick, unforgiving granite. She swallowed hard at the sight when she realized they weren't quite like the dragons she'd already come across.

Rather, like Zane, they had to be Múspellsheimr dragons and Ancients.

She might be exhausted and heartbroken, but seeing dragons born of another world for the first time was undeniably impressive. Thankfully, it wasn't for the immense fire she felt roiling inside them but simply a scientist's curiosity when it came to a new species of anything, never mind dragons.

Relieved they were clearly here to assist them, she didn't understand Zane's deep-chested, vibrating growl moments later. The immense fury that suddenly welled inside him.

"Don't do it, cousin," Týr warned, his growl never more threatening. *"Do not go after King Knud and the prince with my mate in your grasp, or I will rip your throat out and feed it to the lost souls wandering about Helheim."*

Although she initially looked at the dark dragon Zane locked onto, hardly recognizing him as the king who had saved her yesterday, her gaze was inevitably drawn to the huge dark greenish-blue dragon by his side.

"He seems so familiar," she murmured absently. "Why does he seem so familiar?"

"That is the dragon prince," Zane growled. *"And it does not bode well that he seems familiar, for he is a—"*

"Sigdir," she said softly, certain of it. "Just like you and your kin."

Zane didn't reply, and it was no wonder, given how hard he fought to avoid facing off with Knud, his mortal enemy, as well as the king's sons.

"Do you not think I could get past you?" he growled at Åse and Týr when they flanked him on either side, clearly set to keep Zane from heading that way. *"Do you not think..."*

"Hell," Týr groused, sensing the personality shift in Zane at the same time as Athena. One so strong and so enraged, he did exactly what he'd said he would and evaded Týr and Åse with an admirable

maneuver, dropping thousands of feet in mere seconds before he shot out over the ocean in Knud's direction.

Týr roared in rage and whipped after him, but Zane, caught in his darker personality, was fueled by a world of fire and brimstone. Driven by his Múspellsheimr blood, he swooped toward his enemies with such vengeance and a need for death so strong she could smell the stink of it in his soul.

"No," she ground out, something deep inside her fighting it. She refused to let any Sigdir, be they enemy, foe, or even the evil side of Zane, get hurt. A feeling, *conviction,* that burned brightly somewhere deep inside her before she and her shield started glowing, and the air pulsed around them.

Almost instantly, she felt Zane's better half struggling to resurface. A side battling against a half that relished the confrontation he would soon have with his enemy. Yet fortunately, after an internal struggle that lasted several terrifying moments, his better half won out, and he banked a sharp left, heading toward what had become several fronts of dragons, including not just Zane's army but those of Týr, Rafe, and Ulrik's kingdoms, too.

So many, *too* many, for just her.

"Not just you, my friend," Keira said into her mind, clearly stunned. *"But so much more. So very much more."*

Moments later, she understood why and could hardly believe it.

Chapter Twenty

WHILE TÝR CERTAINLY wasn't pleased Zane brought Athena to the Keep, he was relieved when his cousin safely swooped into the Realm with her and threw up the protective dome moments later, allowing Týr and Åse in but predictably, caging Rafe out.

"The enemy retreats, but I will still stand guard outside the dome with our armies, cousin," Rafe said, sounding aggravated but not surprised Zane locked him out. *"Go be with her."* He didn't miss the emotion in his cousin's internal voice. *"Hold her."*

Although tempted to ask Rafe if he'd known all along about everything Týr and Athena had just discovered, he knew better. His brethren would be close-lipped until the end.

"Thank you, cousin." He bit back emotion as he landed in the courtyard alongside Ulrik, Åse, and Keira and shifted back to his human form along with them. *"We will drink to all lost and found when next we meet."*

199

Rafe offered no response but backed out of his mind respectfully as Zane landed with Athena, cupping her in his talon on the ground. More and more dragons landed far and wide and as high as the eye could see on the various spires of the Keep.

"*No,*" Athena said into his mind when Týr started toward her to help her. "*Not yet.*"

Nothing was more difficult than not going to her and wrapping her up in his arms, but he knew she needed to do this and was proud of her for it. Respected her deeply as she set aside her overwhelming emotions and stood on her own, determined to appear strong despite all she had just learned. Despite the tremendous grief, joy, and pride, both were muddling through.

It all made so much sense now.

All had become perfectly, if not painfully, clear.

While Rune's part in all this remained in the shadows, there could be no doubt the shield itself, imprinted with Athena and their unborn child from another life, had led her here at some point and showed her a trail she needed to follow back to it. A path that would help her and Týr remember everything they had forgotten.

He felt rather than saw Zane hold his talon in such a way that he could discreetly support Athena if her legs gave out. Be a wall to lean back on if she needed it. He also knew Åse was doing her best to hold back from going to Athena and supporting her if need be. He saw it in the tightness of his friend's jaw and the hawk-like way she watched Athena, gauging how many steps it would take to get to her if she started to go down.

No surprise, given all Athena had sacrificed for Åse in their last life.

As it were, dragons had been known to bond with humans and protect them back then. Especially if they were as important as Åse had been, given she'd been King Ulrik's sister in that life. Better still, a Viking Dragon King's sister who was an important part of merging dragonkind with humankind.

Ulrik might have been human back then, but being protected by Keira, a dragon Valkyrie, had made him uniquely qualified to oversee a kindred future between two such vastly different creatures.

So, Týr had watched over Åse and bonded with her in that life, becoming fast friends. At the same time, he was protected by Athena, his own dragon Valkyrie. A beast that came to mean everything to him. A dragon he loved and was every inch his mate. His whole heart.

Yet in the end, by divine design alone, Athena could only ever protect him and, in turn, not just dragonkind and humankind but Åse because she was not just important to the times but because she was so important to Týr. His strength even as he was hers, despite how different they were. That was the fate, the pure uniqueness, of full dragons bonding with humans. Of what were essentially aliens to this world forming a connection with those who had long called Midgard their home.

Therefore, the three of them had become intricately connected, and it had echoed in this life when Athena and Åse choked on smoke at various points, undoubtedly linked to what they had experienced during the eruption. Åse when she'd pursued them up the mountain and Athena when she took those last gasping breaths and saved the world.

"Join me, my friends," Ulrik said softly to Týr and Åse, his Dragon King crown aflame as he waited for Athena to stand and get her bearings before they approached her. She had managed it, though, and held the shield proudly yet protectively.

Clearly aware of her fluctuating emotions and how difficult this moment was, Ulrik rested a supportive hand on her shoulder, giving her much-needed strength no matter how strong she appeared.

"You have done well, Athena," he said loud enough, his voice carried to all. "Týr's Valkyrie." He nodded once with approval. "You did so very much for humanity and dragonkind. Saved us all from certain ruin in the distant past at great personal cost."

He might have expected much from Ulrik but not for him to rest his hand on her shield, fall to a knee, and lower his head. This prompted all far and wide to do the same as he revealed what Týr and Athena had so recently realized when she was able to keep Zane from engaging with the enemy.

"We thank not just you, Athena, but your daughter and Valkyrie who came down to Midgard so very briefly to help save not just your mate, her father, but so many others as well," he said. "Now she sits beside Odin in the great halls of Valhalla, helping from afar via both this shield and the love you and Týr have for her. A mighty warrior given an esteemed seat with our All-Father."

Týr felt Athena's heart ache every bit as much as his and wanted to pull her into his arms but knew he had to wait. This moment of recognition was important for all to see and hear. Because every word Ulrik said was true, and Týr couldn't be prouder. Could not be more humbled because of what his unborn daughter had done and where she sat now. The good she would still do from afar via that shield and through her mother.

When Ulrik at last rose and stepped back, a roar of approval for Athena and their daughter arose. Those who hadn't shifted to human form roared fire at the sky in a show of respect.

"We will remain here for most of the day so Zane's people can get to know Athena better and until we're certain the enemy's dragons have fully dispersed," Ulrik said to their immediate circle, including Zane, who had also shifted back to human form. More than that, he had, shockingly enough, bowed to Athena too.

Ulrik looked at Týr. "Once you've made sure Athena is properly known by the people here, join me and Keira in my lair." His attention swung to Zane. "Meanwhile, let us enjoy a drink together, cousin, for you made me and your queen proud this day."

Although he knew Åse was nowhere near ready to show Zane that kind of respect, Týr would always take his king's lead, so he held out his hand to the cousin he'd wanted to end less than an hour before. He'd saved Athena, he would give him that, but had the power of the shield, better yet, the magic of Athena and their daughter to aid him. Athena's life would have meant nothing to Zane's darker side if he could have taken revenge on his enemies.

Truth told, he still didn't trust his cousin as a whole. It seemed far too convenient that Zane had been there when Athena flew off in a dream-induced state and into a past life experience. Moreover, there when she reconnected with Týr's shield in such an unassuming location.

Nevertheless.

If Ulrik wanted to trust Zane, Týr would try to do the same.

"I owe you a debt of gratitude for saving my mate, cousin," he said, his hand still held out to Zane. "You have my thanks and my wings at your back as long as King Ulrik is your one true king."

Although brief, he didn't miss Zane's hesitation before he grasped Týr's arm, hand to wrist, and held firmly. "I will hold you to that, cousin."

When dragon fire flared in Zane's eyes, Týr's vision hazed red in return with his own fire, bringing him back to the moment he and Zane had bonded as boys.

"Might we fight alongside one another as well as we once did against each other," Zane said in conclusion.

They held fast in a slightly too-tight grip that spoke to a continued lack of trust. Toward a distrust Týr hoped he was wrong about.

"But worth paying attention to," Athena said telepathically a few hours later after they finally broke free of her admirers and headed toward Níðhöggr's Ash, the mighty golden ash tree overlooking the Realm. *"There's just something off about him that I can't quite put my finger on. Something that goes beyond his multiple personalities."*

"I agree," he replied within the mind, glad she understood how much this place was essentially Zane's, and he had loyal ears everywhere.

"Quinn woke me yet again." Athena glanced at him with concern. *"She was terrified someone she referred to as 'he' was going to find it, and lo and behold, Zane found me holding your shield."* She shook her head. *"What if he knows something we don't and was biding his time, knowing I would lead him straight to it? Honestly, I don't even know how I got the shield again other than it felt like a part of that place, so my dragon must've tucked it in those rocks until I reunited with it in the way I was meant to."*

"I agree with you on all counts but one," he said aloud as they approached the tree. "The shield is not mine. Not anymore." Knowing the tree in all its divinity would protect them from prying ears and eyes, he stopped beside the trunk and turned her to him. "I merely kept it safe for my mate and our daughter."

Understanding she could finally feel all the emotions she'd been admirably holding back for the past few hours, Athena blinked back tears and tried to speak but couldn't. So he carefully pried the shield from her grip, manifested a light binding around her chest, and strapped it to her back without losing eye contact. Without ever taking away the strength he knew his gaze gave her.

"I cannot tell you how proud of you I am, *brennende liten kompis.*" He wrapped a supportive arm around her waist, pulled her close, and cupped her cheek. "Thank you for keeping me and mine safe in this life and the last. For saving the world because you did." He clenched his jaw and bit back his own overwhelming emotions for a moment before continuing. "We will see our daughter again someday. You know that, right?" He pressed the flat of his palm against Athena's chest. "Feel it."

"I do," she choked out. Her lower lip wobbled as she rested her hand over his. "Not in this life, though, because she can never be reincarnated. Never be our child again here."

"No," he said hoarsely, his heart breaking every bit as much as hers, no matter how proud he was of their daughter. "What she did, the immense power she used when so very young, on top of such a righteous deed, sealed her at Odin's side for all time. A Valkyrie above all Valkyries who can only help from afar because she protects her All-Father now."

"That's good..." Athena gulped hard, and silent tears streamed down her cheeks. "Really good and makes sense because she feels like..." She pressed her lips together, and more tears fell before she managed a few more short words. "She feels like what I imagine an angel must feel like."

Feeling her crumble inside, he scooped her up, sat with his back to the tree, and held her while she finally let go of all she'd been holding in. Let her grief pour out even as the shield at her back filled her with their daughter's love. So much love he felt it too, as the first tears he'd ever shed fell along with Athena's. The bond dragons made with their offspring, even newly formed, was remarkably intense no matter what, so their heartache was very real. Just as real as it would have been had they lived a whole life with their daughter.

There was no way to know how long they sat there wrapped in each other's arms, only that a sense of immense peace filled them when their tears finally dried. An indescribable feeling that coincided with the late day sun igniting the ash in a display of such golden brilliance, he knew their daughter reached down from above, not saying farewell but still right there with them. Always there until they joined her once more.

"Oh, look at her," Athena whispered, feeling the same as she stared up in awe. "How incredibly *beautiful*."

"*Ja*," he agreed, peering up into the glittering branches until his gaze inevitably fell to the woman in his arms. To the beauty shining out of her just as brightly as he asked a question he dreaded but needed to ask anyway. "Will you stay with me, mate? I have thought long and hard on this, and thanks to this tree, you can go back and forth to the future as much as—"

This time, Athena put a finger to his lips as her gaze fell to his face, and she looked at him with so much love it humbled him anew.

"I couldn't be anywhere else but here with you if I tried," she said softly. "So, yes, *ja*, I'll stay and perhaps…"

When her cheeks turned rosy, and she trailed off, the elation he felt at her staying paled to what she had been about to say next. What she hoped for.

"Perhaps yes," he said, his voice thick with arousal and more happiness than he knew he could feel. "I will give you more offspring. As many children as you want. So many that—"

Before he could go on about the astounding count he had in mind, Athena pulled his lips to hers and kissed him so deeply he knew her fertile womb would welcome many indeed.

"*But not quite yet,*" Keira said into their minds. "*Before you two sail off into the rhetorical sunset and fill the skies with loads of baby dragons, we need to talk. There are things you need to know about Rafe and Quinn and a catastrophe waiting to happen.*"

Chapter Twenty-One

"ARE YOU SURE Quinn said that?" Athena asked Keira as she, Týr, and Ulrik enjoyed an ale in their lair a short time later. It was a massive, mostly open-air cave at the very top of the towering Keep. Åse stood guard at one of the larger openings, refusing to drink as she kept watch. "Are you sure she said Rafe isn't to be trusted and that Zane is?"

"She did," both Keira and Ulrik confirmed before Keira went on. "She refused to go into details but was vehement about it. Things are not as they seem any more than Rafe and Zane are."

"And what did she say about her warnings to me across time when she woke me up at both volcanoes?" Athena wondered. "Because I haven't been able to contact her telepathically since."

"Only that she said what needed saying when it needed saying," Keira said on a sigh. "With Rune's help, of course."

Åse muttered something about evasive pain in the ass seers under her breath, but Athena spoke over her, needing to understand.

"And did you ask her why she was being so vague?" She frowned between Ulrik and Keira, coming to Rafe's defense because he deserved to have someone in his corner. "I'm not sure if you've noticed, but her evasiveness reminds me a lot of the very dragon wizard she's determined to call the bad guy in all this."

"We did ask her why, but she wouldn't give us any real sort of explanation," Ulrik provided. "She did, however, say everything was well back in Maine, and all of your friends are now there, including Savannah."

"Well, that explains it, and you know it," she huffed at Keira. "I love her just as much as you, but the moment Savannah comes around Quinn, things get dramatic, and Zoey has to become more of a peacekeeping diplomat than she already is."

When Åse and Týr looked at her in confusion, she explained.

"Savannah and Quinn are like oil and water, and Quinn never thinks clearly around her," she said. "Quinn is a gentle flowing healer who likes to keep things smooth and unobtrusive, whereas Savannah, despite ironically enough being a psychologist, tends to be our wild child who loves stirring up trouble when she's off the clock. She gets bored quickly and can't sit still in her own skin, so to speak."

"A fire lover like you, then?" Åse assumed before her expression fell, and she shook her head, understanding now, like the rest of them, why Athena had been so addicted to fire to begin with. It had been her inner beast's undying need to return to the flames that had taken her daughter from her. "I'm sorry, sister. I did not mean to—"

"It's okay." Athena managed a small, reassuring smile in Åse's direction and meant what she said. "I'm all right." She squeezed Týr's hand, loving him so much it hurt. "*We're* all right."

The pain was still right there, but somehow, some way, their daughter had come through to them beneath that magnificent ash tree and started healing their hearts in ways she couldn't explain. Yet she suspected their inner dragons did because a soothing warmth had remained with them ever since.

Åse blinked away moisture in her eyes before she swallowed hard, nodded once, rested her hand on the hilt of the dagger at her waist, and turned her attention back to scanning outside, undoubtedly to hide a tear before it fell.

"In answer to your question, Åse," Keira said softly. "Yes, Savannah craves fire every bit as much as Athena did before all this happened. Quinn loathes it, and Zoey struggles…in unusual ways with it."

When Åse perked a brow in question, Keira flinched, and with good reason.

"Let's just say when she loves it, she tends to blow things up," Keira said. "And when she hates it, much-needed flames are impossible to come by."

Åse narrowed her eyes, clearly trying to wrap her mind around what that might mean in their day and age. "That sounds alarming."

"Indeed," Athena agreed, cringing along with Keira at what Zoey might be capable of here.

"And she is the peacekeeper in your era, is she not?" Åse wondered.

"She is," Keira confirmed. "Which makes everything happening here even more alarming." Her gaze went to Athena. "Because we can only assume, based on a growing pattern, that she's a Valkyrie too. That all of us are."

"I agree." Athena gave her friend a look. "Yet I'm not like you, Keira, and we all know it."

Athena offered Ulrik a small smile, well aware he had given her more credit than she deserved upon arrival but it was necessary to establish a precedence that the kingdoms beneath him, *not* Zane, were only growing stronger.

She rested a hand on the shield by her side and said a prayer of thanks and love to her daughter before continuing. "What happened in that supervolcano in another life not only took my daughter but my godliness." And she was okay with that. More than okay because it had saved the world as they knew it back then. "Now I'm but a husk of what I once was." She looked at the others. "Nothing more than a scientific dragon shifter, and you all know it."

"No," Åse ground out, clearly upset with that assessment. Dragon fire flamed in her eyes when she looked at Athena. "You are the bravest female dragon I have ever met, and *that* is a power unto itself." Back to being the Åse they all knew and loved, she gripped the dagger's hilt at her waist more tightly as if she meant to cut down Athena's very assessment, no matter how correct it was, and narrowed her eyes. "If you ever utter such blasphemy again, we will fight to the death, and I will win." She jutted out her chin. "Trust me, I will no matter how well you fight, and you *will* battle well, shieldmaiden, having been trained personally by me first."

"I agree." A very loving newly found brother-sister bond lit Ulrik's eyes when he glanced at Åse before he looked at Athena and grew serious. "You will not only win because Åse will train you but because you'll be taught to harness an inner Valkyrie that, while not as strong as Keira's, is still there. An ember we will fan into flames." He gestured at her shield. "Your greatest power, however, remains in that shield for all time. A shield that carries within it not just your daughter but Odin himself."

Athena bit her lower lip and fought emotion as she rested her hand more firmly over it, only for Týr to rest his hand over hers and nod once at her in reassurance that all would be well. She, *they*, the three of them, because their daughter was right there if only in spirit, would be Valkyrie enough to aid in the cause that lay ahead.

"A cause that shows signs of improving despite our enemy's wrath growing stronger by the day," Ulrik continued, following their thoughts easily enough. "Improving despite this dark magical element that's present at crucial times, be it now or in the distant past."

"A dark magical element our friends in Maine should be made aware of, too, because it's, *he*, interfered in both mine and Keira's lives," Athena said to both Ulrik and Keira. "And we have no idea if he's the same internal threat we face here because both the dark magic and betrayer are masculine. I'm sure of it."

"Agreed," Keira said, equally troubled by it because the magic, while definitely dangerous and connected to their deaths in previous lives, also seemed present in moments that steered them in the right direction and ultimately saved many.

"Yet you say there are signs of improvement in all this?" Týr asked Ulrik.

"There are." Ulrik offered a small smile and gestured south. "Rafe and our armies still stand guard despite all enemies having retreated, so let us fly back to your kingdom so I might show you."

"Do we trust Rafe, though?" Åse frowned from Týr and Athena to Ulrik, clearly concerned for their safety. "I do not think—"

"I will trust him until he gives me reason not to," Ulrik replied, steadfast when it came to standing by kin. Also, no coward when it came to another dragon. Never one to cower in fear of unseen enemies. "Come."

Before any could argue, he went to the ledge and shifted, leading the charge with a dragon so large and magnificent Athena, like the rest, thought nothing of obeying him without question. Trusting that he knew best.

She had never felt anything more freeing than embracing her dragon like this. With no craving for fire in her heart. No need for anything but enjoying how it felt to spread her wings and let the cool wind take her. To feel the pure joy of seeing her mate sailing alongside her as they soared with her shield and connection to their daughter, tight in her talons.

Within moments of falling into formation over the now calm seas, not just Rafe and his warriors fell in on either side of them but Týr and Ulrik's dragons, escorting them home to Týr's Lair.

"*Not my lair,*" he said into her mind, staying close. Protective. "*Our lair.*"

She would have cringed at the thought days ago, but everything had changed now, and she relished it more than she could have ever imagined. Wanted to be there with him always and get to know his people.

"*Our people,*" he echoed.

She smiled inwardly. *Their* people.

And she never felt that more strongly than when Rafe's and Ulrik's warriors peeled off just before the lair and Týr's warriors escorted her to her new home. Never felt it more acutely than when they landed and shifted, only for more dragons than she could count to shift, fall to a knee, and lower their heads in respect not to Ulrik and Keira but to her and Týr.

"Mostly you," he said softly, wrapping his hand with Athena's as they entered the huge cave where they first spent hours talking. A cave that now hosted even more weapons than it had originally.

"They've all returned," she marveled. "All the ones I saw in Maine."

"All the ones you summoned to you so you might summon me," he corrected, smiling, pleased all was as it should be again. "Our weapons, mate and fellow warrior. And I will teach you how to use each and every one."

"You mean *I* will and," Åse began, trailing off when she laid eyes on the buffet of scrumptious-smelling food laid out on the head table.

"It is not the food that has her so tongue-tied," Týr murmured. He smiled and pulled Athena close. "But she who cooked it all."

Athena put a hand to heart when she spied the petite, blushing blonde standing by the table, glancing nervously from the dishes she'd prepared to Åse.

"That's Hilda, isn't it?" she whispered out of the corner of her mouth, astonished because she wasn't what she'd expected. If anything, she had thought the woman Åse secretly loved, because she *did* love Hilda, would be every inch the Viking warrior Åse was.

Instead, she was a timid and gentle, albeit clearly loving cook.

And it seemed she had finally crossed the barrier from cook to true love when Åse closed the distance, yanked her into her arms, and kissed her soundly.

"Aww," she murmured, feeling Åse's love as if it were her own. Grateful the Viking woman had finally given in to something she had forfeited for so long. More grateful still that she had found such an accepting community over a thousand years in Athena's past in a Viking dragon kingdom of all things. "How beautiful. How…"

She trailed off when she felt before she saw who had been standing near Hilda. Felt Týr's mother, Maya, as though she were her own mom when she headed their way without his father,

Dagr's, assistance. She wasn't drawn and pale like she'd been before but had color in her cheeks and more strength in her stride.

"Mother," Týr exclaimed, his relief at her improved health obvious as he closed the distance and wrapped her up in his arms.

"My son," Maya croaked, sobbing quietly as she held onto him when she'd thought she would never see him again. "Thank the gods you came home to us."

When she held out a hand while embracing him, Athena understood and went to her only to find herself wrapped up in both their arms. Moments later, Dagr embraced them as well, and for the first time in her life, she felt...family. Not just that, but what it was to be so deeply loved and accepted into a dragon family. It felt like all the isolation, geekiness, and, most of all, loneliness she'd felt her whole life fell away as if it had never existed to begin with.

"Because deep down inside, in a place you never knew existed, you were never alone, my new daughter," Maya murmured into her mind. *"And never will be again because we will stand beside you always. Love you always."*

Little was said after that as celebrations were underway to welcome yet another Valkyrie and her magical shield to their side. Another goddess who would make all the difference going forward. Something none seemed to doubt because look at what had happened on Týr and Athena's quest.

Odin had made very clear, indeed, that he was on their side.

That he fought alongside them if only by shield.

So they danced and sang and ate and loved for hours. Reveled in so much hope, it worried her, and it seemed Åse saw that because she eventually took Athena's hand and pulled her away from the crowd down the very hall they had walked days before.

"Worry is a *good* thing," Åse said at the entrance to Týr's lair. The Viking woman who had so recently been her greatest nemesis grasped her shoulders and looked her in the eyes, never so serious. "Worry is what will keep you vigilant and watchful. It will make you a great warrior and an even better mate to my closest friend."

Having obviously caught everything she needed to through her connection to Týr, Åse clenched her jaw and notched her chin but didn't release her grip on Athena's shoulders despite the tear that slipped down her cheek. One she surely wouldn't acknowledge but spoke to exactly how much she'd figured out.

"Thank you for saving Týr in that life," Åse said, still looking her in the eyes when Athena knew that wasn't easy for her when feeling so much emotion. "Thank you for saving my dragon...your dragon." She swallowed hard. "*Our* dragon."

The details of the life Týr and Åse had gone on to live after Athena destroyed the volcano was mostly lost to them, but it didn't matter. What mattered was here and now.

A new beginning, such as it was.

To that end, Åse yanked Athena into her arms and hugged her so tightly she couldn't breathe, so it was fortunate Týr melted out of the shadows when he did and cleared his throat. Åse held her a moment longer before she stepped away and nodded at the two of them, keeping her no doubt teary face in the shadows.

"Go." She gestured into his lair flippantly, masking an emotional sniffle before she strode back down the tunnel and threw over her shoulder, "And you're welcome."

When Athena looked at him in question, hoping he understood what that meant, he shrugged, pulled her into his arms, and kissed her so soundly she knew he'd been wanting to do it since last night.

Since the very last moment he'd kissed her.

Not losing contact with her mouth, hungry for her kisses, he hoisted her up until she straddled him and walked into their cave, only for them to feel the difference and smile against each other's lips. However she'd managed it, Åse had seen his lair stripped of all female scent except for Athena's, and neither was more grateful as he brought her to their bed, and they made love for the better part of forever.

Or at least that's how it felt as the world fell away, and they loved endlessly, eager to conceive their second child, may she be another female to begin replenishing the population. Then, their third and fourth, desperate to bring as many dragons into this world as possible. Týr would teach them how to battle, and Athena would explore this beautiful new world with them, not with modern-day technology but with the magic of their inner dragons.

A world that expanded to spectrums modern-day science couldn't see.

A gift she realized was every bit as powerful and revealing.

The kingdoms still warred, perhaps more so now than ever, and her friends' futures were unpredictable in all this, but strides had been made. Even though Ulrik's mother and other aunts remained ill, Maya was improving. Growing stronger. And she was a matriarch above all matriarchs, so that meant something.

Had to mean something in this Age of Embers.

Meanwhile, what would happen next was a mystery. Rafe and Quinn stood against each other. He wanted her nowhere near his kingdom, and she thought him the enemy. So perhaps they had been wrong? Perhaps the two of them weren't destined for each other after all?

Whatever the outcome, Zane was more in their corner than he'd been before, and Rafe, as far as they knew, still a stalwart ally. Were they misinformed? Quite possibly.

Either way, they were one Valkyrie stronger, and the weakness that had been plaguing their females clearly wasn't set in stone. More than that, at least to Týr and Athena's way of thinking, as they lost themselves to carnal pleasure, more baby dragons were on the way.

They knew it like they knew the sun rose in the east and set in the west. Knew they would fill the skies with little dragons who would be the next generation despite rumors that dragonkind's end was upon them.

But then, they had learned, above all others, that love had a way of resurrecting all they thought lost. More than that, love had a way of saving the day.

The End

Her Viking Dragon Mystic

What happens when a Viking dragon king and a twenty-first-century woman who thinks each other is the enemy are forced together, whether they like it or not? Find out as *Viking Ancestors: Age of Embers* continues in *Her Viking Dragon Mystic*.

221

Midgard Locations Glossary

Ancient's Lair– Ancient dragon lair.

Cave Catacombs– Network of interconnected caves across Scandinavia.

Cave Harbor– Harbor in Ancient's Lair.

Cave of Memories– Cave born of Forest of Memories.

Dragon Lair– Sigdir dragon lair ruled by King Týr.

Forest of Memories– Powerful forest that captures traumatic events or memories and replays them.

Hel's Rift– A place between Helheim and Midgard for souls waiting to enter Helheim.

Hvergelmir's River– A river in Níðhöggr's Realm that pours from the well that nourishes all life.

Hvergelmir's Spring– Spring that feeds Hvergelmir's River.

Maine Ash– Níðhöggr's ash tree in modern-day Maine.

Midgard's Rift– A place on Midgard for souls waiting to enter Helheim.

Mt. Galdhøpiggen's Peak– Home of the seers.

Níðhöggr's Ash– Great serpent's ash tree in Scandinavia.

Níðhöggr's Realm– (AKA the Realm) Home to Ancients and Múspellsheimr dragons.

Place of Seers– Magical location only those with seer blood can go.

Rafe's Realm– Place of standing stones and caves that only Rafe and Mea can access.

Viking Fortress– Sigdir stronghold first ruled by King Heidrek, then King Sven. Now ruled by King Ulrik.

The Stronghold– A kingdom first ruled by King Bjorn, then King Soren. Now ruled by King Rafe.

The Keep (AKA Leviathan's Keep)– Castle in Níðhöggr's Realm ruled by King Zane.

The Spot– Black spot beneath Mt. Galdhøpiggen where Celtic god Darkness is trapped.

Series Cast

Characters introduced thus far.

Ulrik Sigdir– Viking Dragon King of the Fortress. Most powerful dragon ever born. King above kings.

Keira Sigdir– Ulrik's Queen. Valkryie dragon.

Tor Sigdir– Ulrik's father.

Raven Sigdir– Ulrik's mother.

Týr Sigdir– King of the Dragon Lair. Great warrior, Helheim dragon. Loyal to Ulrik.

Athena Sigdir– Twenty-first century scientist destined for Týr.

Dagr Sigdir– Týr's father.

Maya Sigdir– Týr's mother.

Rafe– King of the Stronghold. Celtic wizard. Norse dragon.

Zane– King of the Keep. Split personalities. Half Múspellsheimr dragon.

Quinn– Twenty-first century healer and friend to Keira and Athena.

Zoey– Twenty-first century diplomat and friend to Keira and Athena.

Savannah– Twenty-first century psychiatrist and friend to Keira and Athena.

Åse– Ulrik's second-in-command. Týr's former partner.

Mea– Ulrik's sister. Powerful in magic.

Rune– Powerful demi-god seer.

King Knud– Enemy king turned secret ally. Father to Jørn and Magnus.

Magnus– King Knud's oldest son. Enemy king. Dragon prince. Unacknowledged Sigdir.

Jørn – King Knud's younger son. Enemy to Sigdirs.

Nine Worlds

Please note that while these worlds do, in fact, reflect those from Norse Mythology, creative license was taken in the world-building of this particular series.

Niflheim (Old Norse: "Niflheimr") means "mist home" or "mist world."—The first of the Nine Worlds in Norse mythology, Niflheim is made of fog, mist, and ice. The darkest and coldest of the worlds, it possesses the eldest of three wells called Hvergelmir, a bubbling boiling spring protected by a dragon called Níðhöggr. It is said that all cold rivers come from this well and that Hvergelmir is not only the origin of all living but where all living will return. When the world tree Yggdrasill started to grow, it stretched one of its large roots far into Niflheim and drew water from the spring Hvergelmir.

Midgard (Old Norse: "Miðgarðr") means "middle earth."—The homeworld of humanity, Midgard is connected to Asgard by Bifrost the Rainbow Bridge. Odin and his two brothers Vili and Ve, created humans. From an ash log, man. From an elm log, woman.

Asgard (Old Norse: "Ásgarðr") Home of Norse gods and goddesses—The male gods in Asgard are called Aesir, and female gods Asynjur. Odin (All-Father) rules over this world and is chief of the Aesir. His wife Frigg is Queen of the Aesir. Within Asgard is Valhalla, a great hall where half the brave souls of Vikings who have died in battle are received to feast alongside Odin. The other half who died courageously in combat go to Fólkvangr, a meadow ruled over by the goddess Freyja.

Vanaheim (Old Norse: "Vanaheimr") Homeworld of the Vanir (AKA–Seers)—An old branch of gods, the Vanir are masters of sorcery and magic. They're also well known for their talent to predict the future. This world possesses healing rock.

Muspelheim (Old Norse: "Múspellsheimr") Homeworld of dragons—Burning hot, filled with lava, flames, sparks, and soot, Muspelheim is home to not only massive dragons but fire giants and fire demons. Ruled by Surtr, those on Muspelheim are forever warring and often threaten those on other worlds. Surtr swears vengeance on many worlds, including Asgard, vowing he will turn it into a flaming inferno beneath his fiery sword.

Helheim (Old Norse: Hel) Home of the dead—The final destination of anyone who did not die in battle. Families reunite in Helheim.

Jotunheim (Old Norse: "Jötunheimr") Home of the giants (Jotuns)—Jotunheim consists mostly of rock, wilderness, and dense forests. Lies in the snowy regions on the outermost shores of the ocean. Because of this, for lack of fertile land, the Jotuns live off fish from the rivers and the animals from the forest.

Alfheim (Old Norse: "Álfheimr") Home of the light elves—Ruled by the god Freyr, Alfheim hosts beautiful creatures called light elves that are considered to be "guardian angels." Known for delivering inspiration via art or music, light elves are minor gods of nature and fertility with the ability to help or hinder humans with their knowledge of magical powers.

Svartalfheim (Old Norse: "Niðavellir or Svartálfaheimr") Home of the dwarves—Masters of craftsmanship and ruled by King Hreidmar, the dwarves of Svartalfheim live under the rocks, in caves and underground. The gods of Asgard have received many powerful gifts from the dwarves.

Previous Releases

~The MacLomain Series- Early Years~

Highland Defiance- Book One
Highland Persuasion- Book Two
Highland Mystic- Book Three

~The MacLomain Series~

The King's Druidess- Prelude
Fate's Monolith- Book One
Destiny's Denial- Book Two
Sylvan Mist- Book Three

~The MacLomain Series- Next Generation~

Mark of the Highlander- Book One
Vow of the Highlander- Book Two
Wrath of the Highlander- Book Three
Faith of the Highlander- Book Four
Plight of the Highlander- Book Five

~The MacLomain Series- Viking Ancestors~

Viking King- Book One

-Her Viking Dragon Warrior-

Viking Claim- Book Two
Viking Heart- Book Three

~The MacLomain Series- Later Years~

Quest of a Scottish Warrior- Book One
Yule's Fallen Angel- Spin-off Novella
Honor of a Scottish Warrior- Book Two
Oath of a Scottish Warrior- Book Three
Passion of a Scottish Warrior- Book Four

~The MacLomain Series- Viking Ancestors' Kin~

Rise of a Viking- Book One
Vengeance of a Viking- Book Two
A Viking Holiday- Spin-off Novella
Soul of a Viking- Book Three
Fury of a Viking- Book Four
Her Wounded Dragon- Spin-off Novella
Pride of a Viking- Book Five

~The MacLomain Series: A New Beginning~

Sworn to a Highland Laird- Book One
Taken by a Highland Laird- Book Two
Promised to a Highland Laird- Book Three
Avenged by a Highland Laird- Book Four

~Pirates of Britannia World~

The Seafaring Rogue

-Her Viking Dragon Warrior-

The MacLomain Series: A New Beginning Spin-off
The Sea Hellion
Sequel to The Seafaring Rogue

~Viking Ancestors: Rise of the Dragon~

Viking King's Vendetta- Book One
Viking's Valor- Book Two
Viking's Intent- Book Three
Viking's Ransom- Book Four
Viking's Conquest- Book Five
Viking's Crusade- Book Six

~The MacLomain Series: End of an Era~

A Scot's Pledge- Book One
A Scot's Devotion- Book Two
A Scot's Resolve- Book Three
A Scot's Favor- Book Four
A Scot's Retribution- Book Five

~Viking Ancestors: Forged in Fire~

Leviathan
Dagr
Thorulf
Vicar
Tor

~Highlander's Pact~

-Her Viking Dragon Warrior-

Scoundrel's Vengeance
Scoundrel's Favor
Scoundrel's Redemtion

~Pirate's Intent~

Rescued by Passion
Taken by Sin

~The Lyon's Den Interconnected World~

To Tame the Lyon

~Calum's Curse Series~

The Victorian Lure- Book One
The Georgian Embrace- Book Two
The Tudor Revival- Book Three

~Forsaken Brethren Series~

Darkest Memory- Book One
Heart of Vesuvius- Book Two

~Holiday Tales~

Yule's Fallen Angel
+ Bonus Novelette, Christmas Miracle

About the Author

Sky Purington is the bestselling author of over seventy novels and novellas. A New Englander born and bred who recently moved to Virginia, Purington married her hero, has an amazing son who inspires her daily, one ultra-lovable husky shepherd mix and two Siberian huskies full of wanderlust. Passionate for variety, Sky's vivid imagination spans several romance genres, including historical, time travel, paranormal, and fantasy. Expect steamy stories teeming with protective alpha heroes and strong-minded heroines.

Purington loves to hear from readers and can be contacted at Sky@SkyPurington.com. Interested in keeping up with Sky's latest news and releases? Visit Sky's website, www.SkyPurington.com, join her quarterly newsletter, or sign up for personalized text message alerts. Simply text 'skypurington' (no quotes, one word, all lowercase) to 74121 or visit Sky's Sign-up Page. Texts will ONLY be sent when there is a new book release. Readers can easily opt out at any time.

Love social networking? Find Sky on Facebook, Instagram, Twitter, and Goodreads.

Want a few more options? "Follow" Sky Purington on Amazon to receive New Release Kindle Updates and "Follow" Sky on BookBub to be notified of amazing upcoming deals.

-Her Viking Dragon Warrior-

Made in the USA
Columbia, SC
25 July 2024

39303825R00135